of loss, despair, and inaction. Through that, though, they find strength in each other to act, and to reach for an outcome that might not be victory, but which isn't entirely defeat. It's a beautiful and nuanced work about love, power, and magic."
—*Quick Sip Reviews*

Praise for R. B. Lemberg and the Birdverse

"The prose is blunt and powerful, the narrative compelling, and the worldbuilding both deep and lightly-sketched, lending an impression of a full world while only touching on what is immediately important."
—Tor.com

"If you enjoy asides on and playing with etymology and language change, if you love fascinating cultural explorations and inventive customs and traditions that feel lived in, this is the story for you. This world feels 'real' in the sense that I can imagine myself wandering into it, and it comes alive in striking and evocative writing."
—Kate Elliott, author of the Court of Fives series

"Soaked in sensory detail, transporting the reader to the world of the tale."
—A. C. Wise, author of Lambda finalist *The Kissing Booth Girl and Other Stories*

"I wish I'd read this 20 years ago. I needed this story when I was first coming into my transness and trying to imagine my own future and what it could be."
—*Corey's Book Corner*

Praise for *The Unbalancing*

"In a narrative by turns gentle and implacable, Lemberg writes movingly and magnificently about disaster, survival, and hope."
—Kate Elliott, author of the Crown of Stars series

"Lemberg's stories embrace truths that we are afraid to confront: that sometimes failure is inevitable, but that hopeful futures can still be found amid the destruction. Despair, love, survival, death, identity, and community are intimately intertwined in the Birdverse. This is one of the most beautiful and important books I've read this year."
—Nibedita Sen, Hugo, Nebula, and Ignyte Award–nominated author

"Reading this book is like diving into the most beautiful language exploring various aspects of human possibility. Everything in this book is so fluid from the words, the setting itself, but also the characters—the way they think, the way they feel, and the way they present."
—*Infinite Text*

"The lush lyricism of the mythology, culture and history in *The Unbalancing* is illustrious and transportive. It's an enchanting world of star lore, magic and gender identity with a roster of heartfelt characters told with such rich prose that kept me rooting for Ranra."
—Tlotlo Tsamaase, *The Silence of the Wilting Skin*

"R. B. Lemberg's Birdverse is one of my favorite places to visit, full of queer possibilities and deep emotional and philosophical musings. In *The Unbalancing* they give us wonder,

devastation, resilience, and love. Lemberg's poetic voice makes even the harshest explorations of loss beautiful and manages to balance grief and horror with hope and joy."
—Julia Rios, Hugo Award–winning editor of *Uncanny Magazine*

"*The Unbalancing* is a story of people and their power, in nature and society, in interactions and relationships, and of consent and belonging, and of failure and hope. 'We gift all to each other,' a wise advisor says, 'nobody and nothing can destroy this.' In the face of catastrophe and deepest fear, Lilún and Ranra learning to strive and share and acknowledge failure brings survival and hope."
—Scott H. Andrews, World Fantasy Award–winning Editor/Publisher of *Beneath Ceaseless Skies Magazine*

"*The Unbalancing* is a heartrending book about power and responsibility; the courage to act and the wisdom to think before acting; about relationships and collaborations that cross differences; about traumas and attempted healings, large and small; about what we can do and what we can save when it's too late to avert the worst. It's beautiful and queer and challenging and tender. And it's a story that could not have been told without Erígra's autistic point of view, without a deep respect for needs like Erígra's, which comes from lived, thoughtful experience. I love all of R. B. Lemberg's work, but I might love this book most out of any of them."
—Ada Hoffmann, Philip K. Dick Award finalist and author of *The Outside*

"*The Unbalancing* is the latest glimpse into the great tapestry of Birdverse, and it's inspiring and contemplative and hot and tense. It finds a group of queer nerds thrust into a place of power, tasked with the impossible, and faced with the legacy

Also by R. B. Lemberg

Everything Thaws (2022)
The Four Profound Weaves (2020)
Marginalia to Stone Bird (2016)

As Editor:

An Alphabet of Embers (2016)
*Here, We Cross: a collection of queer and genderfluid
poetry from Stone Telling 1 – 7* (2012)

A BIRDVERSE NOVEL

THE UNBALANCING

R.B. LEMBERG

TACHYON • SAN FRANCISCO

The Unbalancing
© 2022 by R. B. Lemberg

Interior and cover design by Elizabeth Story
Author photo by Bogi Takács

Tachyon Publications LLC
1459 18th Street #139
San Francisco, CA 94107
415.285.5615
www.tachyonpublications.com
tachyon@tachyonpublications.com

Series editor: Jacob Weisman
Editor: Jaymee Goh

Print ISBN: 978-1-61696-380-4
Digital ISBN: 978-1-61696-381-1

Printed in the United States by Versa Press, Inc.

First Edition: 2022
9 8 7 6 5 4 3 2 1

For Corey

VARIATION THE FIRST:
ICHAR

I leap sideways

Erígra Lilún

When I first came to Semberí's hill, it was frizzed in fog, soft and wispy like ghost breath. The hill was just off the harbor to the north, down a path overlooking the sea. The islands were small enough that I thought I knew every curve and stone here, but I had never seen this place before. I stood waiting for something, I did not know what—a shimmer, and an ending. But the hill continued to stand. Soon enough, the cool breeze pushed the fog aside to reveal a path leading up. Upon the bluish-green hill grew an ancient quince grove—a company of short, gnarled trees, their arms laden with spring blossom.

The air was brisk that morning, and I huddled in my woolen knit vest, my skin clammy with sweat that had cooled in the wind. The boughs of the trees on the hill swayed with the motions of air, the petals rustled and clung to each other, and no other sound could be heard but my own labored breathing, harsh like words that demand to be written down right away.

A poem about the deeds of creation, the goddess Bird descending toward the land with the twelve magical stars in her tail. I had forgotten to bring my notebook.

I went up, and up. All the fruit trees here were quince. I had seen such trees in town, growing alongside the more plentiful apples and pears—but they'd all looked younger. Here, the knobbly quince trees stood side by side, an old guard protecting each other; still fertile, still blossoming. They did need a good pruning. Later that day, I met Semberí.

That was a year ago. I came here almost daily now, often with my pruning shears and my trowel stuffed in the pockets of that same woolen vest, now more tattered for the wear. But this morning there was urgency in my step. Just before dawnbreak, the islands had quaked, knocking me right out of bed.

I had been dreaming—I think—of the Star of the Tides, a desperate blue presence under the wave, contracting and expanding. A scream. I wasn't sure if it was me who shouted. A few books fell off the shelf. An earthenware cup of water cracked by the bedside.

I barely remembered to pull on a pair of pants before running east through the streets of Gelle-Geu. Instead of turning south toward the harbor, I headed north on the narrow, now-familiar path to Semberí's hill. To the east was the angry sea, all muttering water and spittle of foam. I looked up at the grove. The trees were still standing.

Now that I was here, I wanted to stay at the foot of the hill, postponing any actions or conversations, simply to listen. I heard my own strained breathing, and beyond it, the sea lapping anxiously, incessantly at the moss-laden stones below. The hill itself, in my mind, was grasped from within by the roots—the invisible, deep, endless roots of the quince trees. If the roots could speak, I would come here with my notebook and write down the words, then perform that as poetry.

A small notebook was, in fact, in my pocket—I had a habit of stashing them in every piece of clothing. But I needed to check on Semberí, and so, with a sigh, I climbed up the hill to the grove.

There was nobody there.

I stood for a while, waving my arms just slightly in the air, as if I was a tree among others. The earthquake had passed, but the roots of the trees felt shaken, like limbs taken to tremor long after a heart murmur settles. Some of the branches lay broken, but most of the quince trees made it through the night unharmed.

After a while, I crouched. It was always a visceral relief to touch the soil here with my fingers. I inhaled deeply, anchoring myself in the wet smell of the earth, and the delicate, sweet perfume of the quince. Many of the trees still held on to their blooms. Defiant, like me.

At last, a semblance of peace settled in my body. I closed my eyes and called on the magic of my two deepnames. I pronounced each deepname in my mind, first the longer, weaker two-syllable, then the stronger single-syllable, and felt them unfold, like a sudden burst of a strong headache. A few moments later the pain receded, leaving behind a feeling of heat at the crown of my head. I could now envision my deepnames, two strong lights hovering just above my hair. The two-syllable's shining was blended of two smaller pinpricks of its syllables, adding up to a word. The single-syllable's power could not be divided. Having called on these lights, I now could make a line between my deepnames, and make magic. But I often was tempted to let them simply flicker, like tiny light-houses calling ships to the shore.

A named strong, a person with magical power, could hold as many as three deepnames. I only had two, but single-syllables were the most powerful, and rare. The weakest, five-syllables, were almost equally rare, and not good for much. But my configuration was strong.

With an effort of will, I focused my magic on the trees, and traced the roots' journey into the earth.

Not good. The earthquake was over, but the disturbance itself continued.

It came from far below the ground, from the south-eastern direction. I turned that way. The curve of the hill here obscured the sea, but I knew what was there—a vast expanse of water, and in it the Star of the Tides tossing and turning in its restless sleep.

With my magical senses extended, I perceived the star in my mind's eye as a mass of azure deep within the blue of the wave, a tangle of deepnames as wide as the isles themselves. The Star of the Tides, the Sputtering Star, the Unquiet Sleeper—all the names we had given it over the last thousand years. The star was tethered to the archipelago, to the Mother Mountain at the heart of this island, our largest island, Geu. A thousand years ago, it was Semberí who had brought the star to the archipelago, and cast it into the wave.

"You should reach out and touch the star," a familiar voice behind me said. "Extend your deepnames and reach."

You're alive, thank Bird, I thought. *Or—not alive—but something. Not gone.*

I exhaled, and with that relief came well-practiced annoyance.

Why must you always sneak up on me?

Still crouching, I turned to face the speaker. My ancestor Semberí, or more precisely, their ghost, as tattered and intricate as the latticework of foam, floated under the flowering quince tree. They did not look worse for the wear after the earthquake, and I did not care to find out what *worse* would look like on them.

I'm just really glad you're safe.

After a while, I settled on, "I will not reach out." In the year since we'd first met, I must have refused them sixty times. "The star is asleep, and I will not bother it, no more than I would disturb your own sleep."

Semberí moved this way and that, as if in the wind. There was no wind. "You do not want to disturb the star, but it disturbs you. There is barely a year left. The islands rattle while it screams and tosses—don't tell me you don't care, not after you ran all the way here in pajamas!"

"These aren't . . ." I took a look at myself, and sure, I had my day pants on, but also my sleeping top, embroidered with very small cats. I opened my mouth to produce *I dressed in the dark*, then closed it. I squinted at Semberí's subtly quivering form, through which the thickest of quince boughs were visible. "You critique my dress, but you yourself wear nothing but air!"

"I'm a ghost," Semberí replied sagely. "Why would I wear pajamas?"

Something occurred to me. "Do you even sleep?"

"No," they said.

"I'm sorry."

They shrugged away my meaningless apology. "But if I were the Sputtering Star, the Unquiet Sleeper, I'd want you to disturb me."

"You cannot give me the star's permission."

Arguing with Semberí was easy. Annoying, but easy. In truth, I had no idea if I would reach out even if the star was awake, or if I would continue to hide. But it bothered me.

"The star is asleep," Semberí said. "If it cannot consent while asleep, you must wake it, rouse it just enough to bond with it."

"And has the star ever told you that it wanted to be awakened? Has the star, in all this time, been awake even once?" I asked.

"You do not listen, Erígra. I am the first starkeeper, and I know—"

"You say you'd want to be disturbed, but where was your hill before last spring? You hid it away and you unveiled it when you wanted."

"I wanted you to *listen*, Erígra, which is why I opened the hill and allowed you to find it, not because I'm fond of—"

They stopped. Could a ghost catch their breath?

"I do like you, Erígra," Semberí said, slower this time.

"You say you like me, but you keep pressing me." *I, too, can say that I like you, but I never did invite you to call me Lilún.*

For a moment, I wondered if Semberí, too, had an inward-facing name they would share with a friend or a lover—share it with someone who wasn't me.

"I only press you because I must," said Semberí. "We all have our work, and yours is to take this power. Each of the stars must have a starkeeper, to keep the stars safe. This is the foundation of the land, the foundation of our magic, our inheritance from Bird herself and the obligation from her great labor. The goddess brought us the stars so that we could live, and we must take care of the stars. Especially this star. It needs to be safe, to feel safe. Especially now."

"You want me to disturb the star so that I would make it feel safe?" I frowned.

"Not everybody could. But you would, I am certain of it."

Semberí kept insisting that I was the one. When I slept, I could sometimes hear the star. It cried out from the depths of its nightmares; or, on quieter nights, from an easier dreaming that rose against my mind like a caress, then sank back into the water. But these dreams did not make me the one.

The ghost stared at me for a moment, then spoke. Their voice acquired a singsong quality. "The star is asleep because it is ailing. For a thousand years it will sleep, trying not to remember what caused this great

sorrow. The deeds of creation, the great Birdcoming—
you must reach out to the star, Erígra, with gentleness.
It would come to trust you."

Semberí was persistent, but I still didn't know what
they wanted from me. "I have no desire to become a starkeeper, Semberí. I am a poet who likes gardening, or a
gardener who likes poetry, and that's the sum of my
ambitions."

"You are not yet a starkeeper, but this is your destiny.
Ambition is irrelevant. The star can *die*, Erígra. If you
won't keep it, someone else will ascend to the responsibility, someone who will be even worse than your current starkeeper, Bird praise and amplify his years."

It sounded more like a curse.

"Did you . . ." I said. "Did you ever summon Terein to
this hill? Anybody else?"

"No. And yes." The ghost moved back and forth,
dragging their suddenly long cloudy sleeves around in
the air. "Terein is a lost cause. Others . . . came and
went. Some became starkeepers, but never did the
work. Others refused the work. Meanwhile the earthquakes multiply, the earth shakes, the sea . . . Terein
will not last, and the council will choose a successor.
They will send for you then, I'm sure."

"I doubt the council knows I exist."

"Go to Keeper's House," Semberí said. "Seek them
out, introduce yourself, tell them about these dreams
you keep having."

On my own? No, of course I wouldn't. Just the
thought of going somewhere, speaking to people, trying
to explain all this . . . "It's not for me, Semberí. I just

want to tend to the grove."

"You refuse, but it is our responsibility to guard the star and keep the islands safe."

It was yours once, that responsibility. You brought the star here at the dawn of time. Something went wrong, perhaps, and now you're trying to push this on me. I didn't speak out loud, but Semberí heard me, and flinched as if stricken.

"You will understand, one day. If you listen."

"I'm listening," I said, chastised. It was true that I loved the idea of listening, but listening itself was often difficult. Especially when I had to listen to people. Trees were so much better. "I'm sorry. Go on."

"What else would you have me do?" said Semberí. "Abandon the star? Let it fall from my hands and die? Give no answer to its pain? I did what I had to do."

I didn't understand, but I winced at the vehemence of their words. "I'm sorry—"

"You're not." And with a flounce of foam and the spittle of sea-salt drops on my face, my ancestor vanished into the air.

It started to rain, but I knelt back down at the root of the trees. When Semberí wasn't around, I called them *my trees* in my mind. They didn't belong to me, but from the moment I saw them, I tended them. No other trees in these islands stirred me so, even though by my house I'd grown a globe fruit tree, a pair of etrogim, and an olive tree. A beautiful cypress stood by a gathering house I frequented. On the slopes of the Mother Mountain, ancient ship-pines grew proud and tall, whispering their secrets to the winds. Of all the trees on these islands, I loved these quince best. Their great age. Their gentleness. Their blossom. Their poetry.

To tend these trees from root to seed; that was all I wanted. All I wanted.

The earthquakes grew more frequent that spring. Every week we had them, sometimes daily on days on end. The stronger ones knocked branches off the trees, or rolled pottery from the shelves. We were getting used to them.

I came to the grove each morning, as before. Semberí would make a brief appearance to glare at me; I tried to ignore them. Starkeeper Terein never sent for me, and I did not seek him out.

A few months later, when the blossoms were spent and the fruit of the quince trees was new, music suddenly welled from the heart of Gelle-Geu, from the direction of Keeper's House. Somber drums, and the wail of the shofar longhorn to announce the passing of Starkeeper Terein. Then silence. Then, as I was frantically pulling my day clothes on, I heard bells and reed pipes that announced the impending ascension of a new starkeeper. Underneath it all, I felt the rumbling of another earthquake.

I went out. People were coming out of their homes, curious about the news and the music. I didn't want to chat, so I hurried past them to the quince grove. Would it even be there? From the moment we met, Semberí kept pushing me to do their will. If that was the only reason they'd opened the hill to me, wouldn't they close it now?

With every step, a feeling of impending loss gnawed at me, but its sudden, vehement urgency felt pointless. What could I even do now? Plead with the ghost to let me still see my trees if I did what Semberí wanted? Would I even see them? And wouldn't it be too late to acquiesce, wasn't the new starkeeper already selected? I still didn't want to be a starkeeper. I just wanted to tend to my trees, and think my slow thoughts and write, that was all.

Exhausted with worry, I arrived at the path by the shore. The hill was still there, not even fogged—just there, in defiance of my fears, the trees rustling, their roots disturbed once again by the soft rumbling of the earthquake.

I had not talked to the ghost for months; we had just glared at each other. But now, seeing the hill unvanished, I was seized with worry for them.

"Semberí," I yelled, running uphill. "Semberí!" My own voice was startling—loud and hoarse, as if it came from some closed-off, dark chamber in my body. At last, panting, my face wet with sweat, I reached the top of the hill.

They said, "Second thoughts?" Semberí floated close behind me, and their presence, like ice water, startled me so much that I just sat down on the ground.

Your pardon? I wanted to say, but the words didn't come out.

Semberí floated around and half-crouched, half-leaned over me. "It could have been you. The new starkeeper? Erígra, are you even listening?"

"I thought you wouldn't let me in," I huffed.

Semberí peered at me. "I'm glad at least you're dressed, Erígra." Then they whooshed away.

Semberí. I had no will to call after them. I was glad to be sitting. I bent forward and leaned my forehead against the slim, rough trunk of an ancient quince tree. The sensation of bark against my clammy skin brought me back to the moment of grooves and ridges. I got a feeling of age and vitality from the tree, and under its bark, the fruiting heart of sap. I had no idea how long I'd been sitting when Semberí came back. I didn't look up, but I could sense them floating over me, waiting in vain for me to make eye contact. Eventually, they lowered themself. The transparent hem of their garment spread like seafoam over the sparse grass that grew in the shadow of the quince.

"Why do you think I wanted you to be a starkeeper, Erígra?" they asked, almost gentle, as if speaking to a young child.

You probably wanted your blood to inherit. But Semberí must have had other offspring . . .

I looked up at them, and their face was about as welcoming as a storm cloud. "I don't know why you chose me, Semberí. I actually don't know that much about you."

"You would know more about me if you'd asked and listened. And you neither asked nor listened," said the ghost.

"I would listen," I said, a bit too eagerly.

"No, first ask. If you care about consent." They were stubborn, and I still didn't understand why they kept the hill open for me.

"Why let me come here, Semberí, after I refused to do your bidding?"

"What kind of question is that?" The ghost flickered in and out of the salty warm air, and for a moment I was staring right through their head. They said, "You like the trees, and the trees like you. You tend to them. You have a gentle touch. This is why I was sure—" They fell silent.

I muttered, "I don't want to rule anyone." This was my truth, equal or greater than my hesitation about the star's consent. I stared back at the ground, at the grass. If I stared hard enough, little specks of light would dance in my eyes, or I'd draw on one of my deepnames and use their magic to look at the tiny worms and other creatures burrowing in the soil. Some ruler I'd make for Gelle-Geu . . .

"As if these islanders would suffer to be ruled! Each does exactly as they please." The ghost chuckled, a strange sound coming from someone so immaterial. "In any case, starkeeping isn't ruling. In an hour of need we only ask what is needed, and who is needed. The stars are matched to their keepers and we are matched to them, and an hour of need becomes the time for our work. In all other hours, rituals may suffice—but not now."

"I don't understand," I said.

The ghost shrugged. "Do you want to understand?"

I felt sadness, as if I had misunderstood Semberí all along. But despite what they'd said, Terein had been a ruler, and so was every starkeeper before them. The duties of a starkeeper extended beyond taking care of the Sputtering Star. Our people didn't desire daily instruction, but there were things which needed to be done—making sure that groups of magical people—the named strong—came together frequently to purify the water, asking strong builders to build or repair old structures, directing the healer-keepers to those who were sick—and that involved councils, and talking incessantly to people. The starkeeper, the most important named strong in the archipelago, took over these roles. I didn't want to rule anyone. But I would listen, at least, to Semberí. I owed them that.

I said, "I want to hear your story. Please. I want to understand."

"To understand me, you must understand the deeds of creation, the great Birdcoming."

"Please," I said.

"Out of curiosity, what shape does Bird take for you?"

I shook my head. "I've never seen her." Ordinary people only saw the goddess when she came for the souls of the dead, but only the strongest of the named strong could see her—those with three deepnames. I only had two. She would appear to each person in a different bird shape, corresponding to their character and imagination.

"Oh well." The ghost whirled their arms once, then settled. "The goddess Bird came to us from beyond the sky." With every word, Semberí's form became denser, more pearlescent and vibrant, and their voice acquired a familiar storytelling cadence.

"Even before she appeared, we'd heard the song—all over the land we heard it. It was a journey-song, and it lasted and lasted—at times triumphant and cresting, at times it stirred us to yearning, even grief. We did not know who Bird was then, but some of us felt the desire to wander. So we left our newly formed lands, and traveled to the great Burri desert, to the heart of the landmass, guided by the echoing voice of that music in our hearts. There were twelve of us."

Semberí stopped and cocked their head at me; waiting, I guessed, for some acknowledgment, a sign for them to continue. Every child knew the story of Bird and the stars, but few were lucky enough to hear about it from a witness. I wondered what I could ask.

"Did you speak to each other?"

The ghost floated up and down gently. "Not much more than a greeting, but we came together to witness the Birdcoming. The goddess danced in the air, and in her long, flowing tail of azure I saw twelve stars, each different in size and color. As Bird descended, coming closer, the twelve of us danced, and above us, the goddess danced, and the twelve stars shook in her tail. We danced with abandon, with hope and with yearning, knowing and yet barely caring to know that the land was new, not yet firm anywhere, much less in the great Burri desert where the shape of the past and the future kept changing, where sands flowed between us and every movement made music. The goddess danced for us, and we for her."

Semberí fell silent. I shivered, lulled by their story-telling voice into a feeling which wasn't unlike a strong, sudden wind.

I said, "Please go on."

"One by one the stars fell, shaken from Bird's tail by the movements of the dance. Each time, one of my fellow dancers lifted their arms to the sky to catch a star. One after another, the starkeepers left, carrying their stars in their hands, until there were only three of us."

I wanted to know who the last three dancers were, and what had happened, but Semberí fell silent.

"And then?" I said, eagerly.

They switched the subject. "The Star of the Tides was matched to you, and you let someone else catch it. You did not wait for the star. You did not even journey toward it. But you should—I think you should—at least go take a look."

"I don't know . . ." I stared at my hands, the curves and ridges of them, and the blades of grass poking between my fingers. Earth under my fingernails. I didn't remember clawing the ground.

What if Semberí—what if they still wanted—still hoped that I'd somehow wrestle the starkeeper's position from the new person? And if not, would all this end as abruptly as their story, in the middle? The path to the hill would get shrouded in fog, then dissolve into nothingness.

"I have no intention of refusing you entry, Erígra," Semberí said. "And you should stop thinking about it. Come back anytime." A swish of cold air, and I was sitting alone in the grass.

I sat there for what felt like hours, contemplating the curved, ever-changing shadows cast by the trees. The world of the senses cradled me. The cool wind rustled in the branches, and the wind from the sea brought salt and a tangy, bittersweet current I wished I could capture in words. A smell like citrus rind and seawater spray. Beneath me, the wet, heavy pull of the earth, and beneath it rocks, the stone roots of the islands. I hadn't drawn on the magic of my deepnames, but it felt like I had; words had no place anymore, and the world was sharp colors and soft edges. The love of this land filled me in strings and ribbons of light, from the top of the Mother Mountain to its root, the stone and sap of the land delimited by the wave and the slumbering star that floated within it. I could sit here forever, because Semberí wanted me to visit Keeper's House, and I didn't want to go. All those people, and the yelling.

Eventually, I walked home. The streets of Gelle-Geu were full of noise and laughter, with celebrants of all ages and genders dressed in exuberant clothing and adorned with garlands of tiny bells. With every step I felt a little lurch of dizziness and joy, as if my body couldn't decide whether to fall apart or break into a dance.

I lived in one of the northwestern neighborhoods, in a simple stone house. It was a relief, at last, to reach my front garden. Two etrog trees stood here, producing the fragrant, bitter citrus. The word etrog, like others, was brought to the archipelago hundreds of years ago, when Laaguti Birdwing and her many Khana friends came to these shores. I bowed to the etrog trees and stepped over the limestone threshold. Inside, it was quiet, and within breaths, my agitated thoughts replaced the noise of the streets.

Semberí didn't understand why I hadn't wanted to go to Keeper's House. Why not? But *they* didn't go anywhere. *They* did not have to listen to the noise and rattle, *they* did not even have to talk to me until they got to know me, and it took a whole year for them to tell me something substantial. And yet they demanded—expected—suggested that I go to a *party*.

I breathed deep, like my fathers had taught me. Breathing, as ever, helped nothing.

There was no reason for the new starkeeper to see me, and I had no reason to see them. The city was too overwhelming for me to venture out again.

I took off my street clothes and began to comb out my hair. The simple action was soothing. Then I found my box of olive wood, edged in brass and rarely used, and I applied potions and powders until my naturally dark hair was bleached bone-white. It took a long time, and that was good. Gradually, the noise in my mind subsided. I shaved the sides of my head and braided the rest of my hair into five overlapping braids held together with a white ribbon. I was, apparently, preparing to see people and to be seen, but I didn't want to focus on that yet. I needed to add some hair tokens to signal my ichidi variation, but I had never been sure about that, so I let it be. Maybe if I spent more time among people, I could figure out my ichidi variation. Perhaps I could learn to feel calmer around people. Perhaps I could get accustomed enough to another's presence to take a lover again, but it was always easier to go visit the trees.

By the time I got dressed and laced my good shoes, it was almost evening. I was still unsure if I wanted to make the trip up the streets to Keeper's House, but I could at least go out and see if I could stomach it. So I went out.

The revelry outside had become wilder and more joyful—women, ichidar, and men; in groups and in pairs and in triads; mingling and laughing, drinking and kissing. Anybody with deepnames made fireworks. Single-named strong made small balls of light, two-named strong like myself managed flowers and shooting stars. A few three-named strong in the crowd went all out, releasing complex structures that matched their power—bug-eyed fish and fiery ospreys; a serpent of emerald green; an enormous, majestic ship with sails of rainbow. Children were laughing and jumping, their hands outstretched toward the fireworks as if the displays were Bird herself.

It was still overwhelming, riotous, but all my preparations helped me reach a place of quietude inside, as if I walked in my own inner bubble, at a remove from myself and from the world. It was a safe place to be, even though I was moving—my gaze did not linger on faces, and if anyone greeted me, I did not hear. Step by step, I made my way up the streets northeast, to Keeper's House. Beneath my feet I sensed the earth tremble, but it could have been the crowds.

I expected Keeper's House to be guarded against uninvited visitors. Once the large, squat-looking, gray marble building was in my sight, I began rehearsing what I would say to try to gain my admittance. I stopped just shy of the ornate iron gates of the outer garden. The air was perfumed with lilac, out of season but blooming exuberantly. This was supported, I saw, by the subtle but incessant flow of tiny deepnames draped in garlands around the wrought iron fencing.

I leaned closer, as if to look; but I closed my eyes and tried to gather my thoughts. It was hard through the strong scent of lilac, and the afterimages of tiny deepname lights. *I thought I would see if I could be admitted.* No. *Would it be possible for me to*—No. I should have rehearsed this earlier. I shouldn't have come here.

Words kept piling in my mind. *A friend suggested*—Was Semberí a friend? *A relative suggested*—

Someone tapped me on the shoulder, and I startled. One of the gate guards. They smiled. "Were you going to come in?"

"I, um, do not have an invitation." This wasn't at all what I had planned to say.

The guard took me gently under the arm and led me to the gate, where they let me go. "No invitation is needed for you."

"Not for beautiful people, let alone beautiful people of considerable deepname power," said a different guard. They waved me through, and both smiled in unison. I felt uneasy, as if I'd tricked them somehow. Erígra Lilún was nobody's beautiful person, let alone of considerable deepname power. Would they admit me if I had not bleached and braided my hair? I didn't mean to trick anyone, and it wasn't like I would show up to Keeper's House in my earth-tending garments, or worse, pajamas . . .

Still, I didn't want to linger at the gate, so I made my way into the large inner courtyard, and joined the revelers within. With my magical senses—shaken, but if anything, more attuned than before—I felt a veritable vibration of power arising from the crowd. Many people with three-deepname and two-deepname configurations—the strongest of the named strong—mingled here, wine glasses in their hands. I saw people as young as their early twenties and as old as their eighties, and all were good-looking—proud of bearing, bright of eye, and splendidly dressed. There were no children here.

My stomach knotted. Any time now, somebody would want to talk to me. This was a mistake. I should get out of here. Semberí wanted me to take a look at the new starkeeper, ostensibly to make me feel bad that it wasn't me, but oh Bird, how could Semberí think I could *rule* anything? At thirty-five, I was perfectly content with a life of a recluse whose only social outings were poetry readings. At those, I just had to climb on some dais or a chair and read, then try to slip away before anybody could express their opinions to me directly. I couldn't imagine throwing even a much smaller party, let alone the rest of the people-wrangling that being a starkeeper would require. This had been enough of a look.

I was about to turn back toward the gate when I spotted a group of ichidar by a small fountain. They all had their hair done five ways, and the oldest, a large and proud person in their sixties, had brass tokens strung into their five long, thin gray braids. This person's face was round and pleasant, their olive islander skin tanned with weather and wind. They waved at me, and then, unexpectedly, yelled my name. "Erígra Lilún!"

I startled, but surprisingly did not bolt. This person exuded a kind of gravity, a warm centeredness—and without much thought I came closer. One of the younger ichidar thrust a glass goblet into my hands, and many people welcomed me at once.

"I'm sorry," I said.

"Don't be sorry," said the person with the brass tokens. "I'm an admirer of your poetry—I'm Dorod Laagar, shipwright—and this is my crew . . ." As Dorod introduced their fellows, I became again distracted by the tokens in Dorod's braids. The tokens told a story of their life and their journeys through at least three different ichidi variations. First was the deer for ichar—*I leap sideways*—to signal that one was neither a man or a woman, but traveling sideways on one's own path. It was the first ichidi variation, one many ichidar chose for themselves. But it wasn't Dorod's current variation. The deer token they wore was small, followed by a fish for arír, and finally, prominently displayed, a bear for rugár. Animal tokens were out of fashion at the moment, I was given to understand, but I loved looking at these.

"You can have one of mine, if you'd like," Dorod said, amused.

I shook my head. "I don't know my ichidi variation. Sometimes I think I am ichar, but I am never sure. And anyway, I should be going. No offense meant—I wanted to see the new Keeper, but I have no idea how to find them." I cursed my bluntness. "I'm sorry. I'm not used to being in the crowds." I put the goblet down on the striated stone rim of the fountain. I had not drunk anything, but the colors of the courtyard were blending in my eyes.

Dorod nodded sagely, and soon I found myself being escorted somewhere by one of their fellows whose name I entirely missed. We left the courtyard and entered one of the outer rooms of Keeper's House, a dim and spacious chamber with floors of white and black marble and pillars of malachite chiseled to resemble trees. Here was a heavy table strewn with charts, and around it a small gathering of people in animated conversation. I had no time to take it all in, to process, no time to feel anything except for some dark wave, a longing, apprehension, as if I was dreaming about the star, but I was awake. There was a person in her thirties—I knew her to be a woman by her single braid in the custom of those who were not ichidar. She wasn't overly tall, but sturdily built. She was, I suddenly thought, the center of all this—the room, and the conversations.

"Starkeeper." My guide spoke up, next to me, and I felt that movement as air rearranging itself around us. Every tiny sensation was either sharp, or blurred into nothingness. "I bring a guest."

The commanding woman whirled around to face me. Her face went through a series of expressions—a startled joy, disappointment, surprise. Finally, her face smoothed out. She couldn't be called pretty, but she had a striking, commanding presence, and a kind of roar filled my mind. She walked over toward us.

My guide continued, "Esteemed Dorod Laagar asked me to introduce this ichidi to you. The poet, Erígra Lilún."

The new starkeeper was about my age. She was extraordinarily magically powerful—a three-named strong.

Her configuration was not engaged, but I was perceptive well beyond the abilities of my magic. I perceived,
in her mind, a single-syllable, another single-syllable,
and the last, a two-syllable deepname. I wouldn't know
the exact sounds of her deepnames unless she spoke
them to me, and that was not done; but I knew enough.
She held the Royal House, the most stable and benev-
olent configuration known. This exact configuration
could be mine if I wanted to take more power, but I'd
stopped at two deepnames. She had not.

"Well met," said the new starkeeper. She bared her
teeth at me, not quite a smile. "I am Ranra Kekeri."

She gestured toward my guide, and such was the
force of her will that Dorod's friend bowed and all
but ran out. Ranra's eyes, deep brown and perceptive,
locked on mine. "You came here for a reason, and I
would know it."

"You told your guards to admit all beautiful people
with significant deepname power," I blurted out before
I could stop myself. *Forgive me.* But I did not feel like
begging. I stood straighter.

Ranra frowned. "I'm sure that's not why Dorod be-
stirred themself to have you introduced. Or was this an
attempt to matchmake?"

Did she think that I came here to prank her, or, Bird
forbid, to flirt? I did not *flirt.* I'd had my share of en-
counters, none particularly enjoyable or memorable,
and, by Bird, I had never sought out lovers on purpose.
"No," I said. "Of course not."

"Very well. But then what brings you here, Erígra?
I'm waiting."

This, this was the reason I hated parties, hated talking to people I did not already know. Why did I come here? I swallowed my unease, my embarrassment, all of it. Breathed. It helped nothing. "I see the Sputtering Star in my dreams."

Ranra nodded. "Speak on."

I spoke on. "I hear it screaming sometimes. It's having nightmares, and I have—I wanted—I am concerned . . ."

"That I would not keep the star properly?" Ranra's brows knitted together, forming a single long dark brow over her eyes. She wasn't beautiful in any regular sense, but something about her compelled me. She was, she was poem-like, someone I would write about through words of summer storm and thundercloud when I was alone in my room. She was angry, and I did not want her to be angry. From Ranra's mind, a cord of lesser, constructed deepnames extended, fascinating me with its hue, an azure so pure it almost sang.

She frowned. "What are you staring at?"

You.

I said instead, "Your deepnames. The bond you formed with the star, the rope of bright blue that spins out from your mind and then out, curling into the depths of the sea."

Her brows climbed higher, but her mouth untwisted. She stared at me, and I knew all too well what she thought. *If you are so perceptive, how come you're only a two-named strong?*

I ventured an explanation. "I was told that I should take more deepnames, but I would rather not."

Ranra breathed in, deeply, and for her it seemed to work. She seemed less angry, though no less intense, but now I could not guess what she was thinking.

She said, "You are welcome to join my councilors, but I will not discuss the star much longer tonight. This is my party, and I intend to enjoy it."

I did not respond, but she waited for my reply.

"Yes, of course," I finally said. "Thank you." I felt confused, and there wasn't enough air to breathe.

Ranra Kekeri

Here was my moment, my hour. This room, where I'd served as a councilor, gnashing my teeth as the old Keeper waited, Bird knows for what, year after year; this room was mine now. Chiseled of marble and malachite and reflecting hundreds of magical lights, the room was full of people. And all of them looked at me, as if they waited for me to spring into action. A kind of nervous drive, a feeling of glee, filled me from the pit of my stomach to the heart. I could do—anything. Run somewhere. Do something. And yet, I reminded myself, this was a day of celebration. The gardens overflowed with revelers—*my people*—across the three islands who were celebrating *me* tonight. But I was on edge. Impatient. Five years of waiting, Bird peck it. But our islands were prosperous, our gardens overflowed, the people had the freedom of their bodies and their minds and their loves. My people were happy.

This in itself was an issue. Starkeeper Terein had for years refused to do anything, to say anything. *There is no point in scaring the people. They would not believe us. Let them be.* Most islanders had no idea that here, at the inner council, we worried that the star could be dying. The star had been in the wave for a thousand years. Except for some earthquakes, nothing had changed, after all, from the time Semberí had brought the Sputtering Star here and sank it into the sea. And we'd had earthquakes before, so all would be fine. It was nothing.

But it wasn't nothing, and I knew it, and the old Keeper knew it. Earthquakes kept getting more frequent, and stronger. The star was disturbed—I felt it through my newly forged bond, and certainly Keeper Terein would have felt it too, would have woken screaming from the star's nightmares just as I had for three nights in a row. This was a Bird-plucking mess. To figure out what had caused it, and how to fix it, I would first need to convince people who thought we were doing just fine. We were not doing fine. Things were getting worse, and soon would get much worse. The new person, Erígra, knew this.

I just wished I hadn't been thinking about my mother when they were announced.

Erígra looked nothing like my mother. But as soon as I heard the word *guest*, I made assumptions before even looking.

So I looked at Erígra. Again. They were standing by the table with my deepname charts, listening quietly to my advisors Ulár and Somay. Erigra was striking. Their bleached hair was shaved on the sides and braided, contrasting beautifully with the tanned olive of their skin; their eyes, small but vivid in a pleasant face, reflected both intelligence and sadness. I wanted to do things to this ichidi. I wanted to clasp their cheeks and to wind my hands in that hair. I wanted to capture their wrists in my hands, to see that sadness soften into surrender.

Wait. What.

I frowned and focused my magical senses on Erígra Lilún. There was something about them beyond my unexpected but predictable interest, something I needed to understand.

Ah, yes. Erígra was as powerful as me. Perhaps even more powerful than me, although it was hard to say why I thought so, or how that could even be true. My connection to my star, tenuous and fleeting most of the time because the star wasn't awake, surged forward at that moment with a wavelike suddenness, and I tasted salt under my tongue. In that moment, I saw that Erígra Lilún bore the Royal House, same as me.

No, that wasn't right. Erígra Lilún's mind was *shaped* to hold the Royal House. What they held instead was the Princely Angle, a lesser configuration of two deepnames, one-syllable and two-syllable. I remembered my own powertakings. I had taken all my deepnames rapidly, taking a break at the last, but only for a few days as I fought with the urge to take a different configuration. It seemed that Erígra had stopped at two deepnames and would not proceed.

I turned to my advisors. "Leave me. Please. I would exchange words with this poet."

They did as I asked, but not too happily. Soli . . .

Veruma Soli in particular looked sour. I'd promised them all a party, and we hadn't even started on the drinks. Well, there was a party outside. They would manage to entertain themselves without me for a Bird-plucking minute.

When Erígra and I were alone, I patted an armchair next to me. "Sit." I saw them hesitate, because I was still standing, but at last they lowered themself, gingerly, into the chair.

I should've sat, too, but I just looked down at them. It was oddly pleasant.

I said, "You see the star in your dreams."

They nodded, their gaze on their hands.

"Your mind is shaped for the Royal House. It is a very rare configuration. A configuration of power, and stability, and work for the benefit of one's people. I've never once met another, yet you are here, and so am I."

Erígra looked up, their gaze on my chin. "You know that I do not hold it."

"You could hold it if you chose to." I had become starkeeper because I wanted to, and worked for it, and had the power for the job, but I hadn't dreamt about the star before I bonded with it three days ago. "If you took the Royal House, you could become starkeeper, yes?"

"Yes." Their eyes met mine finally. There was pain in them, but it didn't make sense yet, and I wanted things to make sense.

I said, "Instead, I am starkeeper. Yet you are here. Let's see—you think you could have done it better?" Someone was always convinced they could've done it much better than Ranra Crow with her single eyebrow.

Especially my mother, eh.

My stomach clenched in anger, again. This was my day of celebration, the day of my ascension in the eyes of the people. My mother wasn't here, and I didn't want to think about how she refused to come to my ascension revels. Instead of my mother, I was getting would-be starkeepers. Well, only Erígra for now, but perhaps more would arrive to criticize me out of jealousy or smugness and without any desire to offer their work.

It was an unkind thought. It wasn't Erígra's fault that I still, after everything, hoped for Adira—for my mother—to show up. Still, I was upset and impatient. "Why didn't you take the third deepname? Why didn't you reach out to the Star of the Tides?"

Erígra swallowed. Looked back at their hands, and their fingers knotted together, then unknotted. "Even if I wanted to—even if I chose to, I could not be certain that the star was consenting."

Ah. "You *are* here to criticize me. And here I thought for a moment that it could be different between us."

Where did *that* come from? I had found them dashing for a brief moment before this conversation, but I wasn't desperate—I'd never had any shortage of lovers, and my house and my courtyard were full of people who would swoon at my every word. Then why did I—

"I didn't come to criticize you." Erígra made a motion as if to get up. "I'm sorry. I mean you no disrespect. This is not my place. I will leave."

I breathed deeply through my nostrils, steadying myself, angry at myself. I began again, gentler this time, or at least Bird knows I tried. "Please sit. I'm sorry I've been so impatient—if you want to leave, I understand, but I would talk with you."

They swallowed and looked away, and I just stared at the way their bleached braids brushed the shaved sides of their head, their neck. What would it feel like, to grow up so beautiful? My fingers itched. All those gardens full of people, and I would focus on a reticent stranger with a half-finished configuration. Eh.

I forced myself back to the matter at hand. "During that first star-giving dance, the Star of the Tides fell from Bird's tail and into Semberí's hands. That was consent."

Erígra still wouldn't look at me. "Either that, or the star fell haphazardly, and Semberí just happened to catch it. Or the star fell, and as it fell, still sleeping, Semberí ran around like a child playing ball, and caught it."

I shrugged. "It's not like we could ask them how it'd happened."

Erígra made a strange noise in their throat.

I continued, defensive. "We know the recorded history. The starkeepers before me did the same thing as I am doing now."

"It still doesn't make it—" They stopped themself just before the word *right* fell from their lips, but I heard it, anyway. No, it wasn't right that my star only saw nightmares when every other star in the land was awake and conversed with their keepers. It wasn't right that the Unquiet Sleeper's nightmares rattled and shook the isles, it wasn't right that the pattern was intensifying, and it wouldn't be right if, like Terein, I did nothing about it except twist my fingers into a shape of a ladder.

I wanted to tell all this to Erígra, but what came out of my mouth was, "I will always ask *your* consent."

They looked up at me, startled.

Now, where did that come from? The same place as the rest of it, eh.

I pushed on, past my blunder. "This is the reason I became starkeeper in the first place. I will do my best to fix this, once and for all generations. But not today. Today we are celebrating." My mouth ran ahead of my mind, but not by that much, I admitted to myself. This was my day, after all. I decided to give up on pretense. "So, would you like to be touched?"

Erígra laughed, more in surprise than in mirth. "You move fast! We've only just met."

I didn't realize there was a rule to limit my speed. Who would try to slow me down, anyway? The healer-keepers?

I bit my lip. "I do not wish to press you."

"I'm, I'm sorry." They got up from the chair, and I stepped back to give them room. I've made a plucking mess of this, that's what. A pile of congealed guano.

"I came here because of the star," Erígra said. "I'm sure you have plenty of people out in the garden who would do just as well."

"That was uncalled for," I said harshly. "My offer was in good faith."

"I'm only allowed here because your guards judged me beautiful. At your command." Erígra adjusted their hair, and I could have sworn, at that moment, that they weren't disinterested. "In any case. I cannot move this fast, Ranra."

"I understand." I didn't, but people were different.

Still, I wondered if their cheeks would feel hot if I touched them.

I opened my hand, and Erígra walked past me, toward the door. They didn't look back, but I called after them.

"Erígra. Come again?"

"I will, Keeper." They slipped out of my house as if they were running away.

Lilún

I rushed through the crowd in the inner courtyard, hoping to escape without being noticed, but the esteemed Dorod and their crew intercepted me.

"I heard she sent people away to remain one-on-one with you. You can't leave me hanging!" Dorod laughed, and their fellows grinned at me. Someone once again made an attempt to thrust a drink into my hand, but I motioned it away. All I wanted was to go home, where I could feel things in safety. But Dorod had been kind to me earlier, and I didn't want to brush them off in recompense for their kindness. The gossip was all in good fun. I figured I would sooner be on my way if I just responded.

"She, um, asked me a question," I said.

Dorod waited for more, but then their face lit up in understanding. "And did you indulge?"

I shook my head. "I'm not that fast."

Dorod laughed; a deep belly laugh. "She is a rake, our

Ranra. We do enjoy her." Then they peered into my face. "Something eats at you."

Something about Dorod made me trust them. It was, perhaps, the motion of the brass tokens in their hair, the melodious jangling—calming and fascinating at once. Deer and fish and bear. Dorod, too, was striking—not commonly beautiful, but they had this rugár handsomeness, a bigness that I associated with those ichidar who were at the same time women and men.

I spoke, stubbornly. "It's how I was only allowed to approach her, you know, because of my looks. It doesn't sit well with me."

"You are good-looking, Erígra," Dorod said. "You cannot deny it."

"If I decided not to bleach my hair, not to change my earth-tending gear, I wouldn't have made it past the gate."

"Love," said Dorod, "I went to listen to you recite your work three times this last winter. I listened to you read in your earth-tending gear, your shoes wet with muck, your hair uncombed, and it wasn't just because I love poetry."

I wasn't sure if this was such a compliment, that Dorod came to listen to me because of my looks—if they were even saying that. I wasn't sure.

Dorod continued. "Any adult carrying two and more deepnames was admitted tonight, along with many others who wanted to come. Nobody was turned away because of their looks. The more talented you are, the better you look, eh? Muck and all." They winked at me. "But I see you are troubled. I'll let you go—or would you like us to escort you home?"

I refused their kind offer and took my leave, then made my way out of the gate and through the crowded streets. It was darker now, and the revelers, many quite drunk, jostled me. The pressure of bodies, the festival clothes, the smell of sweat and alyta perfume, the joy that emanated from the people, the kisses and moans from every courtyard and rooftop where revelers gathered to share their pleasure—all this made my head pound. This wasn't for me. I wasn't adar, I could imagine taking a lover—but I just didn't move at the speed everybody else seemed to be moving, in Gelle-Geu. The Keeper went from discoursing about the Sputtering Star underwave to *would you like to be touched* in all of five breaths, and I was too buzzy to even contemplate this abrupt transition, let alone form an answer. Perhaps I was too odd to ever find a lover. There was no point of looking for some abstract lover before I could think more about Ranra, and I couldn't think about Ranra when there was so much noise.

Finally home, I took off my festival clothes and walked out to the inner courtyard, full of night-flowering vines and the murmur of water. I had always known I was different from others, and people had known this, too. As a child, I would curl upon myself sometimes, and rock on the floor until the buzzing grew softer. The healer-keepers came, and told my fathers not to worry so much. "They just need the world to be quieter, and less bright. Can you make them a comfortable place to relax?" What I wanted was a pool, so dads Veseli and Meron had labored for weeks to create my quiet place, and dad Genet planted the first vines, and taught me how to tend them.

I immersed myself in that outdoor pool now and floated there, unthinking, under the slowly rotating stars, until the buzzing in my mind receded. The water had cooled off by then, and I found myself shivering, so I called on my two deepnames—just said them gently in my mind—and combined their magic to heat the water. I was told that one should not be able to do this with just the two deepnames, but it wasn't too hard, yet another sign of my unwanted ability.

With my deepname configuration engaged, my magical senses felt clearer. Belowground, beneath the noise of the city, more subtle now that it was night, I perceived the golden glow of the land's deep structure—the magical naming grid, the weave upon which all the known lands rested. The grid felt disturbed to me, trembling. From afar, in the sea, the Sputtering Star tossed in its unquiet sleep, and its rumblings rattled the grid. Even the Mother Mountain's fiery roots seemed unbalanced. I wondered how much this buzz had disturbed me, too, without knowing. *Barely a year left*, Semberí had said. Ranra had never met Semberí, but she, too, knew something.

This was getting worse.

Ranra

Deep in the night the partying finally died, or at least moved indoors. I, too, was indoors, having gotten my fill, more or less, in the gardens. I had looked forward to all of that earlier, but Erígra's sudden appearance and just as sudden retreat had sapped much of the pleasure from the revels. I told myself that there was no point in moping when there was partying to be had. I could mope later, after all, when I was alone.

Now that I was alone, my desire to mope had evaporated. It was late enough that I should've just gone to sleep, but the bond I had formed with my star filled me with jittery, still-unfamiliar energy. I had drunk some quince wine, but it did little to soothe me. I itched to do things.

I started messing with the deepname charts that lay strewn on the table, but got no closer to any answers. The star, a ball of pure magic made of thousands and thousands of deepnames all woven together, lay dormant beneath the wave. I had formed a bond with it through ceremonies. How was this possible unless the star was consenting? It was a being of power more vast than the isles, and my magic was human. If it wanted to reject me, I would be dead. No. For a thousand years, starkeepers here did the same thing—ceremonies to prepare the starkeeper's mind and soothe the Slumbering Star who had just lost a human starkeeper; and then, the activation of deepnames, the slow descent of one's magic below the wave. Strengthened by the ceremony and all my knowledge of starlore, I had reached down, beneath the wave, and I was received. It felt—less than an embrace, to be sure, but an anchoring.

For forty generations it had been like this. Except for Semberí, every one of our starkeepers had gone through the same rituals. Semberí had acquired the star directly from Bird.

Pluck it. Erígra had planted doubt in my mind. Erígra doubted that the star was consenting, but they themself did nothing, just like all the others. A perfect pastime, to sit and stare and wait for Ranra Crow to make a mistake, to be mocked and whispered about to the neighbors.

No. Stop. Erígra wasn't like that, and if they were, I didn't know it yet.

I sucked air through my nostrils, steadying myself. This . . . this thing that happened sometimes, these *thoughts* did not feel this bad since— since Soli had left me. And who was to blame for that? I mucked it up with Erígra too. I myself and nobody else was to blame. Erígra wanted to talk about starlore, and I pounced like a cat at a ball of yarn, without even asking if they had a preference.

As if on cue, Soli—Veruma Soli—entered the room, carrying armfuls of books. She was a tall, athletic woman, her dun hair bleached by the sun. We'd been lovers on and off since we were nineteen, and I trusted her judgment in everything but her choice of lovers, myself included. She nodded at me, then dumped the volumes onto the table. "Here. I found your books. Now go to sleep, Ranra, you're drunk."

"I'm not drunk, Soli." She made a face, and I corrected myself. "Veruma. I'm not drunk, I just . . ." *Keep forgetting that you asked me not to call you by your inner name anymore, eh?* Yes, it hurt that she left me, but this didn't give me the right to misname Veruma, now that the permission to use her inner name had been revoked. "Sorry. I'm sorry." To cover up my feelings, I plucked the *Starkeeper's Primer* from the pile. I had to have read this book a hundred times. There was nothing in it to help me.

"You say you're not drunk," Veruma said, "But I saw you drink more than your share, and you've been awake for days."

"I'm awake, I'm alive, and I need to plucking figure out how to fix this," I snarled. "And yet again here are the five hundred different *ways to consult with your star*," I shoved the book under Veruma's nose. "Here's a chart, there's a chart, turn your configuration this way, form a straight angle, form an acute angle, but none of them say what angle to form when your star is asleep and drifting from one Bird-pecked nightmare to another . . ."

"Ever since you bonded to your star," said Veruma sagely, "you have become even more unsufferable."

At least you have the courtesy to mock me to my face. My spoken response was barely better. "Yes? So why are you here, Veruma? Go to sleep."

Veruma bent over and kissed me on the forehead. "It's dark. Everybody is in bed. Your poet is not coming back."

"This wasn't about Erígra," I said. *Or about you. Or about both of you. Or about me. Eh.* "They talked so dangerously and so deeply, and all I wanted was . . ." Wind my hands through their hair and tilt their head back and devour that mouth of theirs, with which they spoke such things that made my blood run hot and cold at once. "They said they would come back."

"Tonight?"

I shook my head. "They took offense at something." Something about the guards admitting them only because they were beautiful. I shouldn't have ever said this to the guards, not even in jest. Not everybody knew me, and I wasn't just among friends anymore, the whole of the people looked at me now. The thought made me shudder. "I'll explain it to them if they ever come back."

"And the other trysts did not take it off your mind."

"No." Veruma knew me too well, for too long.

I twisted the charts this way and that. "It's not about trysts, it's the way Erígra spoke about my star, as if they could've been its keeper, as if they already knew all of its secrets, and judged me."

Veruma's eyebrows climbed up. "I did not realize that you wanted to be judged."

"I don't want to be judged." I had accused Erígra of criticizing me, but now my mind veered into a new direction. "I also don't want to mess this up. If I'm messing up, then by Bird I hope someone will tell me."

"And if someone will tell you, will you listen? Or will you think they're judging you?"

Why did Veruma need to wheedle me now? I took a steadying breath, then pushed the largest chart toward her. "Look. What do you see?"

"A star of deep blue, charted to show its observable deepnames," said Veruma levelly. "Magical geometrists have been diving into the sea to chart this for centuries, until a full mapping was obtained. This is the master chart made by Ulár Viyann ten months ago . . ." she trailed off. "You know this chart as well as I do; here are the red markings you made yourself, and a few expletives on the reverse."

"I am missing something, Veruma, something obvious. Ulár monitors the star and updates the charts. The nightmares are intensifying, the earthquakes . . . yet the master chart is *ten months old*."

"Ah, no, he keeps separate charts, which he updates with his monthly observations. The master chart is updated yearly, so it will be updated in two months or so . . ."

I growled, "Pluck the goddess, what? Yearly?!"

"By the orders of Starkeeper Terein, who said it was enough to . . ."

My choices here were to continue to rage, or calm down so I could do something.

I spoke in what I hoped was a level tone. "Look, Terein is gone. His soul has been taken up by Bird herself. I, Ranra Kekeri, am Keeper now. I need to know what's going on. And not yearly. Daily."

"Fine," Veruma said. "I'll wake Ulár."

"No, by Bird don't wake Ulár. I'll see his charts in the morning." I rolled up the useless, outdated master chart. Terein must have known something was off, and we kept telling him, didn't we? But Terein didn't want to see the charts. He was avoiding.

Suddenly I had an idea. I got up and looked around for my korob. "We're going sailing."

"Sailing into bed," said Veruma, but she couldn't have been serious. I got my korob, not the dress one I wore for my ascension ceremony, but the good green one, padded and worn into comfort over years of sailing. I fastened the two belts. There was something comforting about putting on a korob. A tradition as old as the archipelago. It said I was ready to face whatever the sea and the wind might bring. Veruma, at least, did not argue.

Soon enough we were striding out of Keeper's House, out of the dimmed and exhausted gardens, through the gates which were unguarded, at this time of night, by anything but my own magical protections. The life in the isles was abundant and prosperous, and not many people bothered with crimes; those of the thrill-seekers who could break my protections were all known to me.

The wind was brisk, rising up from the sea with its insistence of salt and wide-open expanses of water. The cloying heaviness of the night sloughed off me. I whooped and thrust my hands up to the stars that shone exuberant and bold in the dark dome of the sky, as if I too was an ancient starkeeper about to catch a star from Bird's streaming tail.

Veruma was quiet. She had no korob, and the chill must have been getting to her. I wondered where she'd left it. A different named strong would have used their deepnames to warm the air around them, but Veruma's magical ability was not as strong as expected with her Princely Angle. I didn't want to embarrass her by asking if she wanted me to warm her up with my own magic.

I asked instead, "You want to go back, get some clothing?"

"I'll manage," Veruma muttered, her teeth clanging. "For the record, I doubt you'll listen."

"Huh?" I wasn't sure what that was about, but there was no time to chatter. We had reached the harbor. It was a welcome sight, with its shadowed forest of masts against the plush darkness of the sky. Many of the sporting and fishing boats were lit dimly by lanterns both mechanical and magical. Dorod's grand trading ships loomed like sleeping dragons in the night. The seventh, Dorod's newest creation, was new to the harbor. The sea was so dark I could barely see the new ship, swallowed almost into nothing against the gray shadows of the harbor. A few deepname lanterns stole shapes and lines from the night.

The incessant sound of the waves soothed me. Revels had happened here too. Veruma tossed a spent bottle away with her foot and swore under her breath. Come morning, after everybody slept off the revels, the whole archipelago would be outdoors, tidying up after themselves. But, obviously, not yet.

Our sporting boats were anchored close to each other. Mine was newer and sleeker, Veruma's a sturdier, older shape. The prows of our boats were carved—mine with a serpent-head, Veruma's with a stylized mountain lion. The two of us had been sailing since we were small. Sometimes we would race each other, at other times we would sail together. We'd aim for the open sea and watch the sea serpents that came here each autumn to feed on the transitory, delicate shoals of fish. It occurred to me that it'd been a few years since we'd last embraced on a ship, and I wondered if Veruma's suggestion to sail into bed had been meant as an offer. Well, it was too late for that, and I didn't even regret it. She was the one who decided to leave, and we'd been apart for two years. If she wanted me to call her Soli again, she'd need to ask.

I sighed. We'd get together again at some point. We always did. But perhaps not. Thank Bird ours wasn't one of those lands where people expected to take a single lover forever, or take only one lover at a time.

"Your boat or mine?" I asked.

"You should steer, since you have a korob."

Eh. I unbelted the garment and threw it at Veruma. "Here, let's take yours."

"Then why are you even asking?" But she wrapped the korob around herself.

I grinned at Veruma, her face oddly soft in the near-darkness of the harbor. "You'll have to steer at some point anyway, because I'll be diving."

I didn't bother to warm the air around me with magic. I wasn't even cold.

Veruma's boat was a large, sturdy vessel she got as a coming-of-age gift from her mothers. It wasn't a trade-ship, but good enough to take out on a scholarly journey. Veruma took her place at the steering wheel, and something about the tenseness in her shoulders told me she was about to engage her magic. Veruma's single-syllable and a two-syllable—the Princely Angle—was a powerful configuration, but its activation always came at an effort for her. Erígra had the Princely Angle too, but in them the magic sat easily; elegant like spring water in an exquisite ash-fired clay vessel that could contain so much more. For Veruma, each activation of her configuration felt like she was lifting a heavy weight.

I went belowdecks to get diving gear from where we stored it the last time I'd used Veruma's boat, two months ago. A sealskin suit, a pair of goggles made of glass and tortoiseshell, and a diving jar. I put the suit and goggles on, but eyed the jar warily. I'd need to carry it in my arms. And I would need to use deepnames anyway, to seal the jar and keep the air fresh, just a much weaker application than what I now planned. I had another set of gear on my own boat, the suit I dove in when I bonded with my star. I had not put a diving jar on then, either.

By the time I came back to the deck, Veruma had steered us out of the harbor and out into the open sea. She eyed my jar-less hands. "Drunk and overconfident, that's my Ranra. Are you seeking to meet your end in the wave?"

"No, no, and no," I said. "I haven't been drunk for a moment tonight, and if my power cannot carry me safely, I should not lead anyone, let alone keep the star."

"Sure," said Veruma, in a tone that would have made me lash at anybody else. Veruma had earned the right to use that tone with me, so I simply nodded. She knew and I knew that I'd do it my own way, but she didn't have to like it.

My own way wouldn't work for anyone but a three-named strong, but I was a three-named strong. The whole jar thing was much more dangerous than simply using my power. For most people, the jar was the only way. For me, it wasn't. If I lost consciousness and my deepnames became unengaged, the jar wouldn't save me. So I told myself.

We sailed for a while, until from afar I spied a light blue shimmer, as if of luminescent, floating sea life that sometimes animated the wave. It wasn't sea life this time, but my star, reaching out from below; and it seemed quiet for once, almost calm in the darkened deep.

I inhaled, and spoke my deepnames in my mind. As children, we were taught that saying our deepnames aloud to others opened the doors to bad luck. I soon figured out that this superstition simply forced children to strive for earlier and finer control of mind-activation. Still, I hadn't shared my deepnames with anyone, not even Veruma.

I was quiet as I pronounced my deepnames, one after another—the single-syllable, the second single-syllable, the two-syllable. The familiar ritual was centering. Evoking my configuration steadied me, banished agitation, made me feel like myself, assured and focused on the task. I rotated my power, forming and reforming triangles with my three deepnames, then spinning them over my head—until the moving lights blurred into a ball of magic much more effective than any jars of clay or brass would be. Exhaling, I sealed the sphere that would create air out of water around my head. Veruma waved—and I waved back. I wouldn't hear her now.

I waited until she got the boat in position, then dove.

The mass of the boat loomed large until I pushed away from it, then swam just a bit deeper toward the magical mass of blue which was my star. I didn't need to swim very far. No longer quiet, the sea vibrated with magic as wide and as deep as Gelle-Geu. It would be dangerous to come too close. The star slumbered peacefully now, but it could, at any moment, shift into a nightmare.

The bond I'd formed with the star flared to life suddenly, and I began to see things I did not understand.

In my vision, I saw a city ten times as large as Gelle-Geu. It was a city by the sea, a city grown tall with towers of spun glass and lights that hung in the air like flowers. A city where chariots flew through the brilliant air between the hanging lights, a city that sang with the dawn as the wave broke against marble piers chiseled millennia ago with lions and miraculous creatures of the sea, with fish and water dragons, with ospreys diving into the wave.

I moved closer, my eyes still full of that vision. The star's dream? With my magical senses I perceived another reality overlaying the vision I saw. Was this a reality? I wasn't sure, but I felt more than saw the dark water in which I swam. There were indigo tendrils extending from the dense, unquiet core of my star. One tendril was connected to me, another traveled somewhere under the isles, and yet more of them shivered and undulated in the wave. Had these tendrils been charted by Ulár? I wanted to move closer, but something stopped me— perhaps, at long last, some sense of self-preservation.

In my other vision, the stone-and-glass city by the sea began to darken. Humongous fiery shapes obstructed the sky. Stones of flame rained down onto the towers of glass, shattered them in billowing smoke. I heard the screeching of the falling stones, the boom of cracking marble. I heard the screams of thousands of unseen people, and then, the slow, unstoppable noise of collapsing houses and towers.

I gulped water. Around me, the sea roiled.

No! I pushed away from the star's nightmare. The vision of the city faded. Around me, in the dark sea, the magical tendrils flailed around me as I fought for control. My protective sphere was damaged, lessened, but not entirely destroyed. There was less and less air coming in. I screamed in my mind, reforming my grasp on my deepnames. With this magic, I strained to push the water out of the bubble. Succeeded.

What was left of my bubble was much smaller now. I was a strong swimmer, but I had to surface. My diving experience taught that I had to resist the urge to rise up too fast. It took all I had to pace myself as I evaded the tendrils and swam toward the rounded, dark hull of the boat. There was a thin, subtly glowing chain dangling from it, and I grasped that.

"Bird peck you, what was that?" Veruma yelled at me as she hauled me out of the water and onto the deck. "It was calm one moment, the other . . ." Veruma threw her hands up in the air, making an exasperated motion.

Now will you believe me? My head felt like it was about to burst. Veruma's steady, reliable boat was dancing like a child's toy on the wave. *It cannot wait. It's getting worse. I told you so. Still want me to sail into bed and forget about it?*

I spat out water. "Let's get out of here."

Variation the Second:
ARÍR

I frolic in a stream

Lilún

I went to the grove in the morning. It was habit by
now—get up before dawn, walk slowly through the
still-dark streets of the city, softened by the promise of
dawn. On the path by the hill, the mineral smell of the
sea would grow strong as the sun warmed it layer by
careful layer—but that morning I overslept. Between
the buzz of the previous night and my long starlit soak,
getting lost for what felt like hours in my sense of the
land, I had a late start.

I let myself think about Ranra again, on the way
to the grove. How she had leaned over me, as if con-
flicted in her desire to touch and her resolve to give me
space. How she'd sounded angry, as if starlore was not
the thing she wanted most to discuss. Of course not. I
barged into her house with my talk about starlore, and
then . . . Her brows were so bushy and dark, meeting
almost but not quite in the middle. She had some gray
hairs already, and I remembered how they glimmered
between the dark hairs of her single braid. I was smiling.

The way to the grove was familiar, so I followed my feet. In the past I had feared that Semberí would close the hill, but everything felt peaceful this morning. The hill would be there, and Semberí, and I'd tell them. I hummed to myself, thinking about the Sputtering Star and about Ranra's hands, and how she and I had turned out so different even though both of us could be starkeepers. How long it had been since I last took a lover, how insignificant and fleeting all my liaisons had been. How Dorod had called Ranra a rake, and how it was all too easy to believe. What I could expect from Ranra would be fleeting, and I wasn't sure if I wanted anything fleeting.

I became so lost in my thoughts that I ran into Semberí's ghost, and they yelled at me, not quite words—or maybe I did not exactly hear. I got a strange glimpse of Semberi's form—a sense of a mineral purple, as if my body was passing through an amethyst.

Semberí shook themself, and eyed me. "You saw the new Keeper." It wasn't a question.

"Yesterday, at her ascension revels."

"Tell me more," said Semberí, and so I began to tell the tale from the beginning, how I'd bleached my hair, how I'd braided it, how I had met Dorod Laagar and their fellows, how Dorod's brass tokens had jangled. How I still had no idea what ichidi variation was mine, but it wasn't rugár, which was a pity, because a bear token had a very nice shape to hold in one's hand. How I met Ranra. What she said to me. If I wasn't so distracted by my description of Ranra's brows, I would have paid more attention to Semberí's deepening scowl, but they *had* asked me to tell them more.

When I fell silent, Semberí began to flit to and fro, which they did when they were agitated. "She saw something she wanted and moved to take it, just like she did with my star."

Their words shocked me out of my pleasant reverie. "There was no coercion. People flirt, Semberí."

"Not all people," Semberí said. "I don't flirt. I did not think you flirted, either!"

"I, um, I don't flirt. I was mostly just there when she did." Although, to be honest, she more bludgeoned than flirted. I liked that. I'd rather be told outright than agonize for days, wondering whether or not somebody was flirting.

I couldn't help it, the corners of my mouth tugged up.

Semberí's scowl deepened. "I didn't even know you took lovers!"

"I haven't for years and I do not particularly miss it, but I'm not adar, Semberí." It felt odd that I had to defend passionate people—that is, most other people, whose customs and needs felt nothing but strange to me. I wasn't the kind of islander who loved parties and childless gatherings and big houses shared with multiple lovers and children, but neither was I adar. Some in-between place, for which our language had no words. "I just . . . it's not something I worry about usually, but I am not adar. And I didn't know that you were!"

"I am your ancestor," said Semberí dryly. "I invented the word."

"I'm sorry." I wasn't sure why I was apologizing. *You invented a word for people who do not wish to take lovers, but you could not invent a word for me.* Maybe Semberí couldn't even envision a person like me, a person who was mostly adar but sometimes wasn't. And anyway, how could Semberí be my ancestor if they were adar?

They must have guessed my thoughts, because they scowled again. "My daughters were not of my body. There is more than one way to become a parent." They didn't add *everybody knows this*, but I was chastised. Children of the islands had parentages as varied and unpredictable as shells on the shore. I had three fathers, myself.

"Forgive me," I said, now in earnest. "There is nothing wrong in being adar."

"I need neither consolation or approval from you." They circled a small quince tree, and came back. "You say there's *nothing wrong* with being adar, but see, you feel you need to say it. To justify it. It's uncomfortable. The isles overflow with parties. People gather at all times of day and of night, as if there was nothing more important than drink and dalliance, as if any of that will last if the land unravels!"

"The land is not unraveling, Semberí," I said in a placating voice. "In any case, Ranra is working on it. She wants to fix this." I did not expect to defend Ranra either, and my defense of her came out childish, as if wanting to fix was ever enough. As if *fix* was even the word we needed.

I stumbled on. "I think she has good people advising her, and . . ."

"Sure." Semberí shrugged, a strange motion from a ghost. They began drifting away, but I called after them.

"I wanted to ask . . ." Something was bothering me, something that only my ancestor would know.

They stopped, their back to me. From behind, their body appeared even more tattered, and I could see a quince bough through it. "Yes?"

"I wanted to ask if the star was consenting when it fell, or if it fell without knowing and you caught it because you were there, or if you made any conscious effort to catch this particular star when you saw it fall?"

"Oh, child." Semberí turned to face me, and their expression was unreadable to me.

"Please," I said. "I need to know."

Semberí swirled to and fro, agitated. "I began to tell you about the Birdcoming, but you did not listen."

"I listened, but you stopped midway." They made me feel like a child who had to keep begging for a story to be told at bedtime. Semberí wasn't my fathers, and if Semberí didn't want to continue, I had no right to keep begging. "If you do not want to tell me, it is your right."

Semberí stopped swirling around. "When someone falls, you catch them. You take them to safety. That's the whole story."

"I understand," I said quietly.

"No, you don't. For this story, you first must be trusted, and I don't know yet if I trust you."

Semberí's ghostly mouth twisted into a circle with darkness inside. After a moment, their more human visage returned, and they spoke decisively. "I will tell you more." Then they continued, this time without stopping.

"I told you how all but the last three stars fell. How,

in the end, only three starkeepers remained, still waiting, still witnessing Bird's star-giving dance. One of these keepers was a southern man, tall and bald and powerfully built. His name, if you want to know it, was Ladder. The other person was also southern, tall but thin, in a conical hat embroidered with stars. They were called the Starcounter, for in their hand they held a clay tablet with charts and calculations of the stars. This arithmetic had led them from the southern mountain of Keshet, from the first university, all the way north to the heart of the desert. The third of the would-be starkeepers was me, an ichidi from the west, from the unhospitable marsh.

"The tall man called Ladder looked up, his gaze unwavering on the dancing goddess. "'I have never seen a raven so large,' he said. 'Each feather glistens like a blade.'

"The goddess did not look like a raven to me. I saw her as a harptail, the mythical bird that flies over the sea at dawn, when her plumage of azure and aquamarine sings a song as pure as the newborn wave. The goddess's tail as I saw it was a long trailing glory of blue, and the last three stars shone in it. The first was a reddish star made of delicate strands; it looked almost woven. The second star was the color of the tide, and it sang and beckoned to me from Bird's blue plumage. The last of the stars was the largest and darkest of them, and it hung from the goddess's tail like a brooding weight.

"The scholar called the Starcounter looked up, too. 'I know which star is mine, but I'm not yet ready to catch it.'

"'I know,' said the bald man. 'You cannot take your eyes off the star that beckons and clings to the tail of the goddess—that last star, the star of obsidian shards, the one that is full of anguish and wailing. This star would bend all the land to its will, and it is the will of despair.' When I squinted, I saw ghostly ravens and crows dance around him. He terrified me."

Semberí paused in their tale, and stared out to the sea, into some unfathomable distance. Their voice was harsh when they spoke. "You want me to continue?"

I'd heard bits and pieces of this story as a child. Ladder, the headmaster of the school of assassins. The Starcounter of Keshet, with their tablet and their moon goat companion. I didn't know Semberí's version, this thing they witnessed, and the truth of it felt more stark and troubling than any child's tale.

"Please continue, but only if you can," I said as gently as I could.

"I can," said Semberí. Long moments passed before they spoke again.

"'It's not your star that beguiles me,' said the Starcounter to Ladder. 'It's you.'

Again Semberí stopped, as if to gather their thoughts. I did not move, attending.

"At the Starcounter's words, Ladder's face twisted with a feeling. Hunger, recognition, need. He reached out with a deliberate slowness and, without asking, clasped the Starcounter's chin in his hand. 'Is that so?'

"I shuddered to witness this touch, the suddenness and rawness of it. But the Starcounter's gaze was locked on the bald man's. The Starcounter said simply, 'Yes.'

"'Do you want me to leave?' I asked the two of them.

"'No,' they said in unison. 'You need to wait for your star,' the Starcounter added. Neither looked at me. The distance between them was bridged by Ladder's touch."

Semberí fell silent.

"How," I stammered, "how did you feel?"

"Upset. Like I'd asked the wrong question. I asked if they wanted me to leave, but it was I who wanted to leave. I did not come there to witness their embrace. I came for the music, for Bird, for my star. I wanted to leave, but I could not. The Starcounter was right, you see—my star still clung to the tail of the goddess. The Star of the Tides hung close to that Star of Despair that was Ladder's, unbearably close. How could my star not despair? I had a thousand years to think about it."

"I'm sorry," I said.

Semberí shrugged. "I attended to the motions of the dancing goddess, and truths were revealed to me. I felt that the stars had an order to them. The Starcounter's star had to fall next. Then mine. But the Starcounter and Ladder were busy. Talking. Touching. The clay tablet fell from the Starcounter's hand and broke at their feet, but I don't think they noticed."

"Did they . . ." I did not know how to ask this question delicately. "Did they, um . . ."

"No. But it did not matter. They were courting, and I was there too. Was *I* consenting, Erígra? Things are complex sometimes. There are no clear answers. Above us, the goddess danced, but the joy of witnessing her had drained out of me.

"I did not have much of a choice. I could walk away starless, or wait. So I waited."

Semberí stopped speaking, and after a moment or two, they simply dissolved in the air. I stood there feeling sadness, a sense of loss, as if I was being brushed by a soft gray wing. They told me as much as they could. But I still did not learn if the Star of the Tides had ever been consenting.

Ranra

I pried open my eyes and closed them again. This repeated a few times.

I was too queasy to even be furious with myself much. I was somewhere sinking-soft. Had I visited a lover, or . . . ?

My mind was slowly coalescing around the rest of me. I went out with Veruma last night. Too much magic, and being caught underwave, and things shining. She hoisted me into some bed after that. Not Keeper Terein's old bed?

I pried my eyes open for real. Yes, Bird peck it all to pieces, yes. This intricately painted room, all blue and green with striations of seaweed and saltwater on the wall, a jewel of artistic endeavor, was indeed Terein's. Didn't he die here? Why did I need to think about this? I tasted bitterness in my mouth, and my stomach felt queasy, as if I was drunk. Any moment now, Veruma would appear to admonish me.

Or maybe not. This was Terein's chamber. Every morning, someone from the council would come in to reassure him that all was well. I had been on this duty for a few days before they took me off the roster because I couldn't bring myself to tell the starkeeper all was well. On the other hand, I was the starkeeper now, and maybe they would say something else now—? Maybe nobody would come at all, and I would be forced to spend the rest of my days queasy and rolling from side to side in this cloyingly soft bed, unable to escape . . .

The door creaked open, and someone stepped in. I was trying to figure out how to turn without throwing up. The person cleared their throat. "Um, Keeper Ranra, good morning. I am here to report that nothing happened overnight."

"Bird's charred drumstick." It felt good to swear, but speaking wasn't exactly easy. "Look, who are you? Never mind." I still couldn't quite turn, but I found a comfortable spot, and the world wasn't shaking for a moment. I spoke to the ceiling. "I need Ulár. Do you know Ulár? Tall, lanky, single braid, councilor? Get him here and his star charts, the charts I requested *yesterday*."

"Yes, Keeper—"

"I'm not formal. Just go. Please."

Only after the door'd closed behind them did I remember to yell, "And get me some water," but it came out more like a whimper.

By the time Ulár showed up, I'd managed to half-sit, half-lean on the cushions. I hated this, but at least my eye was on the door now. One eye. The other eye was still having doubts about the world, and so it remained closed. But I managed a look at Ulár. He was dressed in his usual informal, grayish-green korob with no decoration, except an embroidered pocket patch with his favorite bird, the woodpecker. I saw the bird right in front of my face, which meant that Ulár, too, was up close. He must have walked over. His long, prematurely graying hair was braided, as usual, into a single braid, marking him as not being ichidi. His arms were full of scrolls, thank Bird. But also, no drink was in sight, and the goddess could not be thanked for that.

"Here," Ulár said, his voice a bit careful. "I was told you wanted to see my star charts." Then he dumped them all onto the coverlet at my feet. "You did not want to hear that nothing happened tonight." This was a statement, but somehow also a question.

"Ulár," I said as reasonably as I could. "I was out all night staring at your 'nothing.' I almost perished because of this 'nothing'. I do not need platitudes, I need facts, I need charts, I need a Bird-plucking drink, I need not to be wearing pajamas . . ."

"You are wearing an old korob," Ulár stated.

I peered down at myself and indeed, I was still wearing my sailing korob.

I chewed my lips. "Did you need to say this just now?"

"I strive for accuracy," Ulár informed me.

I needed water and a change of clothing, and to be dumped into a cold bath, not necessarily in that order, but all I had was his charts, and charts were what I needed.

"What do you have for me?" I said.

"Everything." Ulár looked tense. "Veruma said you

were upset that the most recent calculations were not included in the Keeper's chart you'd received at your ascension, but I updated the chart on the old Keeper's schedule."

I chewed my lips. I shouldn't have been upset, perhaps. Certainly not at Ulár—it wasn't his fault. The old Keeper had wanted one thing, I wanted another, and he would have no way to know.

I sat up straighter. "I'm not upset at you. I'm upset at Terein. It is the starkeeper's job to know what's happening with the star. But he'd only wanted the general charts . . ."

"Even that was too much by the end. Keeper Terein had told me there was no need for the charts at all. He'd just wanted to hear that nothing had happened."

"But you continued charting," I said.

"He told me to stop charting."

I groaned. Then, with an effort of will, I swung my legs over the edge of the bed. Pluck it, but this bed was tall. This motion brought me too close to Ulár, who startled and moved back, then sideways, and began rearranging the charts my motions had disturbed. I tried not to throw up. Plucking Terein. What good would it accomplish to stop charting? But—"If you stopped charting, then what are these charts?"

"Oh, no, I continued charting," Ulár said. "I have been charting for years, at the same interval, every eight days."

"Oh." It deserved a stronger acknowledgment, but all I could muster was, "Good."

"Got to keep pecking." He did not even smile. "So, do you want to see?"

"Yes!" I wished we could move to the council chamber and spread the charts on the table there, but the coverlet it was. I had to twist to follow his motions, but my queasiness seemed to be improving now.

"I can explain everything to you." Ulár unraveled a few scrolls, then quickly rolled them back again. "The biggest scroll right here summarizes what I found in the eight-day charts. It is updated to three days ago. The next regular charting is in five days. These smaller scrolls are separately charted events like earthquakes. I do them after something happens. They are numbered according to year, season, and month. These are the most recent ones, I have more in my rooms."

He unraveled a small scroll, pointing out something that looked like a tendril drawn around connected dots. "This is from last week. These tendrils are new, they started appearing a few weeks ago, so I have been charting them separately."

"I saw these tendrils last night, when I dove to look at the star. Do you know what causes them?"

"Probably?" Ulár was in his element now, and speaking a bit too fast. "Let's think about personal magic for a moment. A person without magical ability can hold no deepnames. A person with magical ability can hold between one to three deepnames. The strongest of the named strong have three deepnames, which allows us to form a variety of beautiful triangles . . ." He cleared his throat. "The star, of course, is a joining of tens of thousands of deepnames, which means a possibility of forming not just triangles, but almost infinite geometric shapes—yet it mostly retains the shape of a ball . . . the extremities of the star, however, are usually formed from longer deepnames which tend to cluster at the edges of the star. These longer deepnames then combine into chains or tendrils in an interlocking pattern—I have a chart on this somewhere . . ."

"Ulár," I said. "When I asked what causes the tendrils, I did not mean the geometry, I meant why now."

He peered at me. "The tendrils are thrown out of the central sphere of the star when a disruption occurs. The center of the star is composed of short deepnames, and that remains more or less stable. But the longer deepnames at the edges of the star are shaken into dynamic new forms; for example, tendrils."

"But why . . ." *Why are they being shaken like that? Why not before?* But it seemed pointless to keep asking him *why* when all he wanted to talk about was *how.*

I rubbed my forehead. This was too much geometry, and too much talking right now. When I ascended, I'd said that I did not need nor want anybody to wait upon me, but maybe a little bit of waiting would have been helpful this morning. "This is all great, Ulár, but now I really need a cup of something. For example, tea. Water would do."

"I understand." A shadow passed over his face. He reached for the scrolls on the bed. "I'll update the master chart on your schedule, just let me know how frequently you want it. If at all."

I touched his arm. "I am not Terein. I'm just hung over. Mostly from magic." I wasn't drunk last night, but now I was facing the consequences of literally all my actions—drinking, dalliances, diving—without even a memory of enjoyment to help me.

"Listen," I said, "I want to be updated daily. Or weekly, or whenever you have an update. Let's talk more later. No, please leave the scrolls here."

For a while after Ulár left, I stared after him. Then I unrolled a random chart. Here was the star at rest, in its familiar shape of a ball. A ball in which the most powerful, single-syllable deepnames clung at the center, and the weakest, the four and five syllable ones, formed the soft, wispy outer layers. Dense in the middle, soft outside, still very much a ball—unless shaken. Was I shaken? No, I needed to get up and get dressed and go find my tea and my people, but it was hard to stir myself, and I detested that.

My stomach churned. I unraveled another scroll. The star's magical connection to its human keepers, the tether made of interwoven two-syllable deepnames, led here, to Keeper's House. Led to the Keeper, whoever that happened to be; led to me.

Ulár's chart showed me the star's second tether—a longer deepname chain that ran from its heart, through the earth underground, bypassing the city to the south. This tether led to the very heart of the island of Geu and of the archipelago itself—to the Mother Mountain. The city's southwestern edge nestled against the mountain's snow-capped height. As a child, I would run to her, run up her pine-covered slopes, daring myself to run without stopping until I collapsed, exhilarated and breathless, hugging her to me, being gathered into her in turn.

The second tether had always been there, but now I wondered why it was needed. The *Starkeeper's Primer* said nothing about stars being tied to their lands. I needed to understand this. Groaning, I slid off the bed, more or less uneventfully. I wasn't picky about beds until now, but they would need to get me a new one.

Lilún

Semberí dissipated, their story only partially told. I closed my eyes and felt the movement of salt and air on my cheeks, postponing the moment when I would think about what Semberí had told me. The quince boughs swayed in the wind, and I, too, moved like the trees moved, my arms outstretched like their blossom-laden arms. From this place, from the hill, I could see the vast water, just slightly stormy under the endless, roiling wave of the sky. The water above and below me was soundless. The sea crashed against Semberí's quince hill without as much as an echo. As I swayed, lulled by the rhythm of the silence and my own deeply rooted green self, lines began to float in my vision, words of secrets or poetry unspoken.

> *I could not abandon the Star of the Tides in its pain*
> *I knew it was dangerous, yes,*
> *but this was a thing I could do. Wait for it, cradle it, carry it*
> *Perhaps if it slept for a thousand years, someone would understand*
> *I opened the grove to you, knowing*

The Unbalancing

There was so little time, and yet you refuse—

I snapped out of my treeing self, no longer blissful. There was no sight of Semberí. It had been a year since Semberí had opened the hill and allowed me tend to the quince grove—but they had only just now shared some parts of their story with me. They'd wanted all things at once. They wanted me to act, to lead, to run somewhere, and they also wanted me to come here, to listen to them. To ask questions. To understand.

I liked the second thing so much more. Ranra could run and lead, and I could come to the hill. We would take years, Semberí and I, getting to know each other, speaking around each other. Swaying in the wind. Semberí said we only had a year, but I hoped for more time. This was my pace, and theirs, too, and eventually we would share the stories, say the things, stay together in silence. I liked that thought.

Ranra, now, the thing with Ranra was different. Remembering our meeting, I shuddered with a feeling I could not quite name. She was so fast, and angry, and also somehow like a warm storm, and thinking about her made me shift from leg to leg and rub my cheeks. Not at all like a tree.

I had promised to visit her. Why did I do that? She'd asked, and I'd said yes, and now I had no idea what to do. It would be best to do nothing at all, to stay in the grove while the sun rose higher over the wave, but my feet had different ideas. By the time my mind caught up with the rest of me, I was already downhill and walking toward Keeper's House.

Ranra

Long story short, I put on clean clothes and found some tea. A promising beginning to the second day of my keeperdom, but at least I felt less cruddy. I had told my people that I would take care of myself, and as of late morning I managed to get out of bed, get dressed, and think a thought or two about how the star was connected to the Mother Mountain. Incredible efficacy.

I scowled, and then laughed. My people would need to help me, and I would need to let them. I wouldn't be like Terein, I'd told myself. Terein was lazy, and so he had to be served hand and foot because he thought himself more important than anyone had any right to be . . . But this magic was more exhausting than anything I'd known. Was this what had made Terein so ineffective? Was he perhaps not lazy but exhausted? Afraid?

I would need to think about this later. Now I was going to the mountain.

I left the rooms, forcing myself to feel more energized with every step. After all, Ranra Crow's great virtue was her obstinacy. They could laugh all they wanted, but this was true.

Greeting people here and there, I managed to escape Keeper's House almost unbothered, until at the very gate, Veruma caught up with me. She looked exhausted, too, as if she hadn't slept well. She wore a light green tunic embroidered with silver, which harmonized beautifully with her deep olive skin; on her wrist, she had a large silver bracelet with an open-beaked crow. I had given it to her years ago. Was this supposed to be a hint? Did she . . . um, did she like last night's misadventure so much that she wanted to flirt? She felt so familiar to me, and frustrating, and wholly Veruma.

"Good morning," I said. "I'm going out."

Veruma's eyebrows knit. "They told me you could barely move."

They told you I couldn't move, but nobody bothered to bring me a cup of tea. Including you. I was grumpy and I knew it. It wasn't Veruma's job to serve me tea, nor anybody else's, and Bird knows I made that clear before I ascended.

"I'm fine." *If you could stop being so protective and yet so annoyed with me at the same time, we would still be together.* "Is there something . . . ?"

Veruma got distracted by a sudden loud miaowing from below, where a large orange cat with a swirl on one side was weaving between her legs, demanding attention. She bent, absentmindedly, to pet it. I resisted the urge—it would bring me too close to Veruma, and this wasn't the time.

"Is this your cat?" I asked. "Or Keeper's House cat?"

"Don't change the subject, Ranra. Where are you going?"

The cat walked over and rubbed against my leg, and I gave in and crouched to pet it. Veruma and I were too close, except for the swirly buffer of purring cat.

I shrugged. "I need to see someone."

"Ah." Veruma's face looked like she'd bitten into a raw etrog. "You're going to look for your poet."

"What?" I forgot, in the excitement and strangeness of last night's events and this morning's charts, that I wanted to think about Erígra Lilún. But now, of course I remembered Lilún's—Erígra's—appearance, their hair, their dreamy expression . . . their words . . .

Veruma snorted. My face must have been easy to read.

Wait. There was something going on here. With her. "Are you jealous?"

"When we selected you Keeper, you promised to steer these isles as Terein never did." Veruma spoke with more and more heat. "You promised to consult with the council, to look at charts . . . and instead, you get drunk and run away from Keeper's House to poke at dangerous magics or speak to people who have nothing to do with the work."

The cat, deciding wisely to escape the battleground, slinked away with a swish of their tail. I opened and closed my mouth around *Stop telling me what to do.* If I said that, a moment later we would be yelling at each other like two teenage girls on the brink of our first breakup. It was the one thing in which we had plenty of practice.

I turned my face away from Veruma's, to put some distance between us now that the purring ginger belly was gone. "We've chased away your cat."

"I've never before seen this cat." She got up, and so did I. We stood facing each other, no longer too close.

You are jealous, and I don't know why you're jealous

two years after our last breakup, and we aren't trying to get back together right now, and we aren't trying to drift even further apart when there is work to do. That voice was only partially the Keeper's voice.

"Veruma." I made my voice as low and steady as I could. "I reviewed the charts, and now I am going to the Mother Mountain. You can consult with Ulár, and he can show you the same charts, but you will not stand in my way."

"I . . ." She looked at me oddly. "Listen, I'm sorry you feel you need to go . . ."

Pluck it. When I felt sad, or upset, I would go to the Mother Mountain. Veruma knew it, and she knew that I knew it. But I wasn't going to the mountain to cry, I was following the charts. I could explain myself, and we could get into another argument, or I could not.

I did not change my tone. "When I return, we will convene the council and discuss our situation."

Veruma didn't argue, but she followed me to the gate, and out of it. "You should let people come with you, Ranra," she said. "You are Keeper now."

"I am Keeper now," I echoed. When I took the job, I thought I would have no power except the power vested in me by my people. But I had the connection to the star, and the obligation to my star. This nobody would take away from me, neither by love nor by pleading.

From the north, on the path above the harbor, a lone figure was approaching Keeper's House. I narrowed my eyes to see better. A handsome person with bleached hair and an elegant tilt to their head. It could be Lilún. Erígra. They were coming here.

My cheeks warmed up, but nothing good would happen if I stayed. If my duty could not be swayed by Veruma, it could not be swayed by Lilún.

"Look," I told Veruma, "Erígra is coming here, I think. So here's your chance to talk with them and figure out whatever you need to figure out. I have work to do. Just please tell them to come later." Without waiting for Veruma's acknowledgment, I walked through the gate and headed southwest.

Lilún

Every time I walked out of the circle of Semberí's grove, the world changed. The difference was slight, and perhaps for someone else it would be easy to miss, but it was all the more jarring for me. It was as if I'd stepped over an invisible line. The smell of quince blossom ceased, and the breeze that blew gently through Semberí's grove was transformed into a stronger, bluer, colder wind. The sea looked different, too, darker now without the sheltering lattice of boughs. The sandstone path toward Geu Harbor and Keeper's House beyond it felt different, too—wider and newer than I'd remembered. I was tempted to turn back, to hide from the world in my grove, but I wanted to see Ranra again.

The sun was ascendant, and from afar, the polished gray marble walls of Keeper's House shone in the sun, glistening with veins of green. I didn't want to meet people, so I chose the slightly longer path that led above the harbor, rather than through it. Seven tall ships stood out among the mass of smaller boats. They had multiple masts and sleek prows carved with serpents and cats, and each was painted in a single color of the rainbow. The last of them was new—still unpainted and scaffolded. I hadn't made the connection at first when I met Dorod Laagar, but now I was curious.

There were so many rumors about those ships. I'd heard that Keeper Terein ordered those built as funeral vessels, to scatter his ashes over the slumbering star. And I'd heard that the ships were Dorod's idea. Dorod planned to take them trading, back east over the sea to the springflower city of Iyar, where the locals did not honor ichidar and where powerful women could be forcibly stripped of their deepnames. But the trade was good—lush fruit and deceitfully smooth plum wine, and razu ivory carvings and embroideries of the goddess Bird as a swan and a swallow, and even more famous weavings that came from the Burri desert itself to be traded through the ports of Iyar.

Yet the tradeships had stayed put through Keeper Terein's funeral, and nobody rushed to sail to Iyar. Dorod's folly, some had said; or that Dorod had too much influence, too many friends, too much time on their hands. Yet others had said that a sea-serpent people lived in the wave to the northeast, north of Iyar, near the marshy land called the Coast. When all the ships were ready, Dorod and their crew would set sail over the wave to meet and trade with these people. I didn't know what to believe and I should have asked Dorod, but I wasn't good at those things—did not even remember the ships when we met.

I snapped out of my reverie at the faraway sound of voices. Two people stood at the gate of Keeper's House—a tall one and a shorter, sturdier one. I stopped and shielded my eyes against the sun's glare, to try to see them more clearly. Two people, yes, and an orange blob on the ground some distance away, perhaps a cat. The shorter person abruptly began to walk, faster and faster—in the opposite direction. I thought I recognized the set of these shoulders, the energy of these steps—was this Ranra? Should I run after her?

Was she running away from me?

I just stood there, trying to make sense out of this, but all I accomplished was frozenness. I had no idea what to do now, or where to go, and perhaps my eyes were lying to me and it wasn't Ranra at all. I'd only seen her once before.

The other figure, the tall person who stood still through the first few minutes of my hesitation, suddenly waved their hand at me and beckoned me closer. I took a step, and then another, and soon enough I stood outside the now familiar garden gate. There were no guards to examine me for beauty. The person who stood here was a tall, cool woman in a light green tunic and indigo pants. She had an elegance about her, and an aloofness that masked something more, some intense feeling that was watery and remote like a cool blue-gray spring wind.

"Hello, Erígra," she said.

I had to have met her before, at the party—or at the council inside. She was one of the people with Ranra, yes. I wasn't good at faces or names, and last night my gaze was on Ranra anyway, but now my cheeks felt hot. "I, um, I'm sorry. I don't . . ."

The stranger smiled slightly, and again the feeling of cool, watery elegance intensified. "We met last night, but briefly. I am Veruma Soli, one of Ranra's councilors."

"Was that Ranra just now?" I blurted. The orange blob I saw from afar, indeed a cat, chose that moment to bump into my ankles.

"Yes. She says to tell you to come back later."

I froze again. She did run off, and did not care to even wait for me. Why would she wait for me? I was a stranger, a nobody.

Veruma shifted, and I realized I was looking at her boots. I forced myself to look up, and her face had cleared; I did not realize she had been frowning before. "It's Ranra," she said, with a tone of mild annoyance. "You're trying to figure out what's going on, and she's already running somewhere doing things. Don't say I didn't warn you."

"Oh?" I wasn't sure I was fully following the conversation.

"Ranra and I have a long history."

Was she saying that they were lovers? I couldn't tell. I tried to read Veruma's face, but I wasn't ever good at that. All I saw is that she had the Princely Angle, same as me. One syllable and two syllables. I had no idea if Veruma wanted to show me her magic; it didn't feel much like mine.

"Don't worry," Veruma said. "Ranra and I are not together now, and it wouldn't matter if we were. She's not

singular. Neither am I, though I usually can't be bothered these days."

This was a kind of conversation islanders loved to
have at gatherings, and I could never figure out how to
react or join in. I couldn't remember when I last took a
lover, let alone discussed my preferences anywhere.

Veruma peered into my face. "Are you nervous?"

"I'm always like this." My gaze slid away from hers. "A
friend said I should have competed for the Keeper's seat,
but I can't even talk to people."

Veruma laughed. "You're fine. I like you."

I had no idea what even to say. *I like you too?* I didn't
know her well enough to tell. After a moment of awkward silence, I went for the one thing I knew how to
talk about. "You and I have the same configuration, the
Princely Angle."

"I wouldn't be able to tell. So no, not the same." She
sounded colder now, and bitter.

This is how it always went. I said something and it
wasn't the right thing to say, and people got upset, and I
had no idea why. Lately when I saw people, it would be
to read poetry at them from a dais somewhere, and go
home. There was also Semberí. I was sure I'd offended
them too. "I'm sorry . . ."

"Don't worry," Veruma said again. "It's always like
this."

"I do not want it to be like this." I still did not understand anything, just that Veruma was unhappy. She
shrugged, and we took awkward leave of each other.
When I started on the path toward home, she waved
at me again.

THE UNBALANCING

Ranra

I broke into a run. I didn't care if someone saw me. Out of the Keeper's neighborhood, south, away from the usual paths people took up the mountain—then a sharp turn to the west. The world blurred into green and blue; the air buoyed me. The far-off call of the mountain reverberated in my ribs, as if my heart would leap out of my chest like a fish. I had not been there for months, but there was no fixing that now. My feet knew the way.

I pushed myself. Faster.

I didn't call on my deepnames, but as I ran, my connection to the star flared clear and bright through my body. And I thought I could feel the other bond under my feet, tetherlike, connecting mountain and star.

Up the slopes I ran, driving thoughts away with every reverberating step. Not now, not now, not now.

The pines on my Mother's southeastern slopes had been culled. I saw the stumps, the roads left by carts and workers. Some of this seemed very recent, labor almost finished, but still I saw a cart here, a tent there. The logging would not be noticeable from the city, a nod to the mountain's pristine beauty that shielded and framed Geu's landscape—but the mountain felt changed.

If I stopped to investigate, I would stay here. I pushed on, higher and higher on a running path I used to frequent when I was a schoolgirl. I passed a few other runners who waved at me. The higher I went, the wilder the mountain became—the heavy smell of pines warmed up by the sun, the boulders, the rustle of small animals I did not see, my leaping breath. My own mother—

The mountain was my mother. This I knew. Here was the care I needed.

I would not reach the summit today, but I kept ascending until my ears hurt and my breath grew labored. I should have stopped, but I kept at it, my speed driving thoughts and fears away until my whole body sang. At last, as if without thinking, I ran off the path and flung myself on the ground.

With time, I became aware of the stones digging into my stomach, and pine needles under my hands. Below me, the Mother Mountain's body, breathing, angry, frightened. Perhaps I was imagining this. Underneath it all, was the mountain's guarding and welcoming magic. And yet below that, the tether.

Please, Mother. This wouldn't do. I needed to talk to her. This always seemed to work, even if she could not answer me.

I seemed to be alone. And if other people heard me, well, what could they do? Complain that the new starkeeper runs up and down and talks to stones? I snorted. *Well, beats Terein, who ran nowhere and talked to nobody.* But this was not the time for these thoughts.

I turned my face to the side and spoke out loud.

"Mother, I came here because I always come here. Because I miss you. Because I do not understand, and I need to understand. What does the tether mean? Were you bound like this from the beginning? Who put it there? How much time do we have? What do I need to do?"

I waited for my answer, but nothing came back. No clarity. Only the warmth of her, the play of light in the branches of the pines, the scant wind. The feeling of being loved by something so vast, so unending, the feeling of her embrace. Acceptance, even back when nobody else had embraced me yet. Her love, unhesitating, steady, casting its shadow upon Geu and upon the sea. A sharp, urgent cawing of a crow overhead.

Bit by bit, my breathing grew calmer. I unclenched my fists and lay my palms on the dry, warm slope of her. My whole body relaxed.

After a while, I got up and bowed deep to my mother, then started descending. I felt better—more centered and brighter, even if I was no closer to clarity. My resolve would carry us through.

Halfway down the slope, something tugged at me. An exhale of old magic, a silver thread of nearly extinguished deepnames. I didn't notice them in my rush to run upward, but now the faint shimmer beckoned me. Did the mountain show this to me? In any case, I followed, out of the shadow of the pines to a smooth, lone rock that jutted out of the slope, overlooking the sea to the southeast. There, the water had turned dark. The waves roiled. My connection to the star flared again, disturbed and agitated, nightmarish. The star was not awake. The star had never, in our memory, been awake.

I turned away from that vision to see what the mountain wanted me to find at the end of the faint thread of silver. It was a little chest, buried under rocks and sealed with the Keeper's seal. I probably should have waited in case it was dangerous, or brought the chest down to Keeper's House with me, but patience was never known to be my thing. I dug into my pockets, found the Keeper's seal, and stuck that into the lock.

The chest snapped open. Inside it was a letter scroll, unsigned but clearly written in Terein's small, squiggly script. He must have come here personally, so this had to have been deposited before the latest onset of his illness, at least a year or so ago. The letter was addressed to me.

I know you come here often, so you might find this. I do not want anybody else to read it.

I unrolled the scroll further. There was more writing on the other side.

You think I oppose your selection, but if you are reading this, you have ascended.

I do not oppose your selection, and neither do I welcome it. The Keeper's job is meaningless now. There is little time left. The star is tethered to the mountain. When the star goes, so does the mountain.

This is not solvable. Nothing can be done, and it makes no sense to alarm the others. Let them live while they still can.

I got up and tucked the letter into my pocket, fuming. How much like Terein to guard his despair like a secret, something for me to discover and share in, like it was his legacy. Pluck that. Maybe time was running out, but Terein's despair had been just that—despair. Despair had its place, but I was a leader, and this was not my path. I would not despair before I put all my power into the work. Perhaps not even then.

And I would not do it alone. This had been my mistake, and Veruma was right about that. I would need the help and knowledge and the company of others. I would seek out Erígra; they seemed to know things. Ulár, too. And Veruma, and the others. Terein had avoided the council, avoided his people, sulked in his rooms; but I would not. Many people would be willing to help in this work if I asked, or even unasked, if I only allowed them to help.

Here, after all, was my clarity. I found it with my Mother, just as before when I came here. I would need to grow stronger and better if I wanted to lead, but the road ahead wasn't hopeless. The road ahead was my work.

Lilún

In the evening a few days later, I fixed my hair and went through my box of ichidi hair ornaments. I wasn't going to attempt to see Ranra again. If she wanted to talk, she would not have run off. Surely she had forgotten about me by now. I, too, had forgotten some things—such as the fact that I'd promised to give a poetry reading tonight. The keeper of Under the Tree sent a messenger to remind me that, a month ago, I had committed to perform there, and it felt easier to just go along than to ask for a different night. Besides, I'd written a few new drafts, and I could read something. It would take my mind off other things.

There were modern, jeweled tokens in my box, but also old-fashioned ornaments given to me by my fathers when I was fifteen, after my second and last powertaking—a single-syllable deepname to complete my Princely Angle. Powertaking seemed less hard back then than other things, such as gatherings. I wanted to declare myself ichidi, but that involved going to a party or a gathering where I could be witnessed by people. *Be sure to dress neatly and, most importantly, do your hair,* my fathers had told me. *It's courage you can wear.* It had sounded silly before I tried it, but it worked every time.

Ichidi tokens, though, continued to befuddle me. I wore all of them at once, back when I went to my first gathering, to show that I was ichidi but had not yet chosen my variation. Twenty years later, my ichidi variation remained elusive. Perhaps I had simply refused to think about it.

Tonight, I put aside the jeweled tokens and went through the brass ones, thinking about Dorod—their assuredness, the solidity of their age, and their laughter. I would wear the old-fashioned brass in Dorod's honor. Perhaps I would see them at Under the Tree tonight.

Should I wear all five, or . . . ? Having touched them one by one, I set aside the bear, the deer, and the serpent. My hand hovered over the arír fish. *I frolic in a stream.* A variation of joyful flowing, of falling in love, of art and imagination. Dorod had worn that one, though smaller and less prominently displayed than the bear. The arír fish was a thing from their past—a token of moving gracefully between the different gendered states. I could see how arír could be a precursor to the bear, which meant that Dorod had abandoned graceful fluidity for strength and groundedness in the worlds of women and men, belonging to neither. The rugár bear was not my way, but neither, I decided, was the arír fish. I was neither fluid nor solidly positioned between polarities.

That left me with the zúr turtle. I traced its brass back, and the small head that poked curiously from its shell. Like the bear, the turtle token felt hefty in the hand, rounded and meditative. I had not thought much about the turtle before, except that I did not understand it. But now it seemed appropriate. It wasn't an intuitive, immediate attraction, but a slow understanding that moved at its own pace. The zúr turtle's ancient saying went, *when others rush to divide and declare, I carry my world.* The turtle was a world in which the distinctions between women, ichidi, and men did not make sense, and that in itself, I now clearly saw, was an ichidi variation.

By the time I finished pleating the turtle token into my hair, got my pages packed and left the house, the sky was starting to darken. I was going to be late, but it didn't matter now; the air was ripe with promises and secrets, and the breeze from the sea was warm. The city had cleaned up nicely after the revels, each person coming out—some joyfully, some grudgingly—to do their part, but the luster of the celebrations had not quite worn off. I saw sprigs of blooming alyta flowers hung over doorways, the wide triangular clusters of blooms exuding a peppery, sweet smell. Lovers would be out and about tonight, and I wondered if I should have chosen a different poem to read, but those lovers would not come to listen to me.

I followed the flow of the streets, left, right, left again; moving closer to the sea, but not quite as far as Geu Harbor or Keeper's House, until at last I spotted a familiar tree. It was a cypress with a beautifully winding, bare trunk strewn with candlebulb lights, their delicate magics flickering like fireflies in the warm evening air. A two-storey house of whitewashed limestone nested companionably under the cypress. Outside, in the courtyard, two dozen people were mingling and talking, but all turned toward me when they saw me. These were my would-be listeners, who had given up on my arrival and taken their drinking outside. I waved, tuned out the greetings, and snuck quickly indoors, into the familiar semi-darkness and the comforting smell of well-oiled wood.

Soon enough I stood on a dais slightly above the gathering space. People were coming in, and if I looked, I would, perhaps, recognize familiar faces. But my custom at readings was to ignore the existence of my audience, or else I would not be able to read at all.

I cleared my throat and peered into my papers. This poem was very rough, and I had no idea how it ended. Whatever had possessed me to choose it? I should have read one of my older, more polished pieces . . . perhaps I could recite something from memory?

In my agitation I yanked at my hair, and the zúr turtle fell into my palm. I thought it had been more securely attached. I did not mean to unbraid it, but the turtle's weight and shape in my hand felt reassuring to me, like it was all right to move at my own pace. I closed my hand around it.

In the dimness of the gathering space, people were now growing quieter. I saw them as shapes, as shadows, nothing more. I looked back at my page. Took a decisive breath, which did not quite steady me.

"This is called 'Remember Semberí'."

With every word I spoke, my voice grew stronger, as if it no longer belonged to a lonely and hesitant person, but came instead from the dawn of time when I was one of the first starkeepers attending upon Bird.

> Remember Semberí
> the star of azure as it fell
> into their outstretched hands,
> and in that moment
> they saw their house destroyed
> before it was even built.
> But they could not abandon
> the Star of the Tides to its pain
> even knowing that it was dangerous;
> this was a thing they could do—

wait for it, cradle it, carry it
over the turbulent tide, coming here,
to plant the star in our wave.
Perhaps if it slept for a thousand years,
somebody, who could not be me,
before everything ends
would discover gentleness

I kept reading the unruly, half-formed lines, until even those lines faded in my vision. I lifted my head. "That's as much as I have. I'm not sure how it ends." While people began clapping, I sat down at the edge of the stage, my feet dangling, and accepted my customary globe of citrus water from the owner of Under the Tree.

"This went well, I thought. *Did* it go well?"

The proprietor shrugged. "It was a very fine piece, but perhaps . . . it would have been better with a bit less doom and gloom, especially, um . . . considering how we just had the new Keeper's ascension . . ."

He motioned somewhere, and I had no idea what he meant until a familiar voice cut over him. "Don't worry on my behalf. I won't melt from sad poems."

Ranra. She wore a hooded korob—very stealthy—but apparently the only person who did not recognize her was me. I couldn't even look at people until after a reading. But it seemed I was glad to see her, because warmth spread onto my cheeks. "I thought you forgot. Or did not want to see me?"

"I asked Veruma to ask you to come again." She winked at me. "Then I was incredibly patient. I waited for two whole days for you to show up. I could have waited even longer, but Dorod told me you would be reading tonight, and I was curious."

I couldn't help myself. "What did you think?"

"You're brilliant, and you know it," she said. "With just the right amount of doom and gloom."

Her hands twitched just slightly; I wouldn't have noticed if I hadn't been avoiding looking at her face. So I looked at her face.

She was as before—condensed and commanding and not quite pretty. Her eyes, all darkness and secret promises, locked on mine. "Shall we get a table?" Her attention made me feel warm and giddy and not quite sure of myself, but Ranra waited with me until I was comfortable.

"Yes," I said. "Let's."

We got a table in a far corner of the hall, almost dark enough for comfort, though I was sure that everyone would be watching from the corners of their eyes. It was an islander thing, that curiosity, but I wondered what Semberí would think if they saw.

I shuddered, and my hand opened. The turtle token I still clutched rattled onto the table. Ranra caught it before it could slide off, before I even had a chance to move. She pushed the turtle toward me and took her hand away, then watched me as I picked up the brass token, still warm from Ranra's hand. Or so I imagined.

She cleared her throat. "I want to talk." Then, suddenly, she got up. "In a moment."

I had no idea what was happening, except that Ranra had a speed that I did not possess. I wondered how much her configuration energized her. Three-deepname configurations were rumored to have that effect. Then, there was her connection to the star. As I contemplated this, I started to unbraid my hair so that I could reattach my zúr turtle properly. It was delicate work and difficult without a mirror, and I got so caught up in the moment that I did not notice when Ranra returned. But she was back. In front of us were two glasses of chilled etrog juice. I looked at her watching me struggle with my hair, and my cheeks warmed again.

"What?" she said. "I will not touch you without your consent."

My lips twitched, hopefully only slightly. "Is this why you sought me out?"

Her lips twitched, too. "No. And yes. Maybe. I want to talk."

I gave up on trying to reattach my turtle. It was time to admit that I had no practice in affixing tokens. And I gave up resisting my feelings, too. "You can touch me. If you still want."

Her hand covered mine almost immediately. Her grip was strong without being forceful, her fingers calloused and rough and utterly thrilling. She leaned closer, and I tried hard not to swallow.

She said, "I want to talk about the star. My star. I was bothered—worried—by what you said about the Star of the Tides not consenting. So I went out to the sea, and I saw . . . I saw something I didn't understand. I think it was the star's nightmare. A vision of a dying city. When you spoke earlier about Semberí's vision, I wondered . . . I wondered if they had seen it too."

"I believe," I said, "that Semberí saw many things. I'm

not sure if the star was ever awake, but it fell into their hands. They did not chase after it. I believe the star came to them."

Ranra said, "This situation is dangerous."

"I believe you are right."

Her grip on my hand became stronger, then it eased up. "It's not a matter of belief, Erígra. It's so bad that Terein gave up and refused even to see the measurements that Ulár—I think you saw him the other day, when you came to see me—he charts the star, and every time there is an earthquake, he measures how strong it is."

"How—how do you measure something like this?" I stammered.

"Vibrations. Ulár came up with this. He's a very fine magical geometrist. You can ask him for particulars when you see him again."

"How bad?" My voice sounded small and frightened to my ears.

"Bad," she said.

"How soon?" *Semberí told me we had a year . . .*

"Soon." Ranra frowned. "We have a year, maybe two if we're lucky. Maybe."

So it seemed both starkeepers agreed on how much we had left. This wasn't encouraging at all. I did not want to believe Semberí—it could be just another story they told me—but I couldn't shrug both of them off.

"And then what?" I did not want to know, but I asked anyway.

"The Slumbering Star's nightmares have become more frequent, and with it the earthquakes. I am not sure why this is happening, but there is a tether—two tethers—one that binds the star to me, to people, I think, and the other that binds the star to the isles . . . to the Mother Mountain. If something were to happen to the star . . ." Ranra fell silent, brooding over her own vision.

"What can be done?" I asked.

"I'm not sure yet. But I know I want to fix this. Do you want to help me?"

I put my other hand on top of Ranra's hand holding mine. She looked startled, but made no motion to disengage.

"Keeper," I said formally, "you asked me if I could be a starkeeper myself, and there is something to this. I, too, studied a bit of starlore." I learned from the ghost of our star's first starkeeper, but I didn't want to tell this to Ranra. Not yet. "Keeper, I need to be blunt. I do not like this word, *fix*, that you keep repeating. The stars are alive—they have pain and stories, they have journeys and dreams—this I'm sure of. The stars are alive even if they are asleep. The stars, when awake, can consent and withdraw their consent, and they can converse with their keepers. The stars are people, and you do not fix people."

Ranra digested this in silence, her right hand still held between mine. Then she placed her left hand on my left hand, topping the mountain that our hands had made. "Very well. What should I say instead? Do you like *heal? Mend?*"

"I don't know." I sighed deeply. "I offer so little . . ."

Ranra disengaged her hands, and I felt a sudden pang

of loss, but before my feelings could develop further, I saw that she was only lifting her glass to her lips. She drank the juice, then said, "I noticed that you're not that much into wine."

I smiled at her, genuinely glad that she noticed. Most people just made assumptions. "It is enough that I help the quince grow."

She grinned at me. "And write beguilingly about doom and gloom."

I grinned back like a fool. "Please call me Lilún." It was my inner name, and one I rarely offered to anyone.

"Lilún." She rolled it around in her mouth. I hoped she would say it again, but she just smiled at me. Then I felt her hand on my knee, under the table. Her touch was too sudden, discomfiting, but then both steadying and thrilling, as if I just dove headfast into the sea.

She asked, "Is this good for you?"

Before I knew it, I was nodding, my heart thudding birdlike against the cage of my chest, and her hand moved on, to my thigh. She held my gaze, but I could no longer look at her. I could not speak. I wanted—I did not usually—ever—go this fast, we barely just met, but I wanted—yes, I wanted—I wanted her to go on, I wanted to feel what it was like to be carried along in the summer storm of her, even if this would be fleeting. Because it always was. I would be devastated when she left. But even knowing that, I did not want to stop.

"Ranra," I gasped. "Let's go elsewhere."

She said, "I forgot that you didn't like gatherings."

"It's not just that, it's . . ." I stumbled. Even if I liked being watched, I would not want to be watched after what Semberí had told me. It felt wrong now. Islanders didn't much care about such things, but Semberí found it distressing, and I cared about Semberí, and it wouldn't feel right after that story. Besides that, no, I did not like gatherings.

Ranra stood up, and smiled down at me. "Then let's go."

Ranra

I took Lilún's hand and led them out of the place. They didn't want to be seen, but everybody had seen us, the islands being what they were. I wasn't sure why this bothered them, but I went with it. Outside, under the cypress, casual drinkers and poetry lovers grinned and waved at us. A few had suggestions, not too softly spoken. I gathered that they were rooting for Lilún to get some, but Lilún wanted this private. So I took a step toward the onlookers. My grin, I hoped, was not quite like the sun.

I said, "Shush."

They shushed.

I grinned again, aiming for something a bit more pleasant, but who knows. In no time, we were out from under the tree. I led us aimlessly, gleefully, through the fragrant dark air, looking not so much for direction as for a shady nook among houses fallen quiet for the night, and found it soon enough. It was an ancient stone wall covered with vines grown soft in the darkness, framed by the shadows of old trees. Lilún's hand tightened in mine, and the sound of their breathing was like thumping blood in my ears. Above us hung the summer sky with all its navigating stars, but I needed no star to show me the way. I backed Lilún to the wall. They felt so eager, and at the same time they let me lead, and I was glad I had not drunk anything. I was already flying. "Is this good for you?"

"Oh, yes," they sighed, and I sunk my hands, at last, into their hair. I was going to pull their head back and kiss them on the lips, but then they made this wonderful, throaty sound. I kissed them on the neck instead, and I drank their sighs and their shudders. Their skin was salty from sweat and warm with their arousal, and now they clutched me, pulled me closer. My tongue found that delicious hollow at their throat.

The sound they made was too loud for the place. Somewhere above us and to the left, a cat miaowed loudly, in an oddly familiar way. I blinked. Was that Veruma's cat? Someone yelled cheerfully at us to take our business elsewhere, on account of it bothering the wildlife.

"Cat yours?" I yelled, undaunted, toward the voice.

"Cat's their own!" the voice yelled back.

I tore myself away from Lilún, and laughed. "So, where are we going?"

They laughed, too, a bit shaky. "I thought I would take you home, but then you were so certain you knew where you were going." Their hands clutched my sides.

I murmured, "You can still take me home."

"It's farther away now." But they took me by the hand and led me this time, and in the end, it wasn't far at all.

Their house was simple, but the gardens were lovely. The inner courtyard was framed by limestone walls overgrown with vines of pale purple nightflowers in bloom. In the middle of the courtyard was a stone pool, large and tranquil, surrounded by yet more plants whose shapes I could barely make out, even though the stars were bright.

"Can you do that again?" Lilún asked, and it turned out that they wanted me to press them against the wall.

"Do you have any cats I should know about?"

They snorted. "No. I cannot be trusted with any living being that isn't rooted in the ground."

"I trust you."

I pushed them into the masses of soft, fragrant flowers whose names I didn't know, and we locked our lips for the first time. Everything felt sharp and soft and full. My body framing theirs. A stray vine tickling my neck. I pressed Lilún even more to the stones, and they slumped against me, as if some long-held tension released in them.

I tore myself away to ask, "Do you like this?"

"Oh yes." They sighed. "I like being restrained. It makes me feel brighter."

"How do you like it?" I nibbled their ear, then whispered, "Do you like it with rope? Do you like it with magic?"

"Ranra, I . . ." They moaned and shuddered as I licked my way down their jaw, then down their neck. My hands were busy, too. I could not stop tasting them, touching them, squeezing them, and I felt full to bursting with power. Lilún said, "Yes, please . . . I want to try it with magic . . ."

I could not believe that I'd waited almost two days for this. Fool. I should have run after them immediately after we met.

I called on my deepnames. Many people said that calling on short deepnames hurt, but I felt exhilaration, not pain. Wielding the Royal House was my favorite thing in the world—and it was certainly true in passion. The Royal House was mighty, and yet it could be so tenderly applied. I made strictures of light in which to hold my lover, hold them gently and firmly while I let my hands roam. And then Lilún engaged their magic too. The Princely Angle was a scaled-down Royal House—less strong, less expansive, but Lilún had a capacity to hold more magic, which I'd already noticed in them. Veruma had the same configuration, but being with Veruma felt different. She was more assertive than Lilún, but also weaker, and I did not want to think about Veruma now.

I tightened my structures and turned them around until Lilún sighed into them, floating deep in their trust, and I was going to make them beg for more.

Later, we ended up naked in the stone pool. Lilún floated gently on their back. I leaned against the pool's polished edge, contemplating the reflections of the stars that wavered in the water. I should probably have been going, but I didn't want to go anywhere. Perhaps if I lingered some more, they would invite me to stay the night.

It was hard to make out Lilún's face at this angle, so I moved closer. They looked a bit cold. A bit forlorn. It made me sad, too. Perhaps they were one of those people who felt sad in the aftermath of passion, or perhaps this hadn't been as brilliant for them as it had been for me. I wanted to take care of them, anyway.

"Are you cold?" I asked. "Would you like me to heat the water?" My magic became unengaged at some point during our private revels, but I could call it again, and there were perks to being a three-named strong.

They seemed to think this over. "I think I'm all right for now." And then, "Weren't you going to leave?"

That stung. "If you want."

"I—but Ranra . . ." They half-emerged from the water, peered at me. "I assumed it would be a fleeting thing for you . . ." They were close enough that I could touch them if I reached out, but I did not.

I tasted sadness in my mouth, citrusy-bitter like an unripe etrog. "Why, Lilún? Why did you think I would want something fleeting with you?"

"Maybe because you're so set on beautiful people, and, I don't know, you can have anybody, there's no reason for you to pursue me past this." They sounded so glum. A bit lost.

There was an easy way out of this. I could get angry at their assumptions. I could jump out of the Bird-plucking pool and get dressed and be on my way. I'd walk the sadness off, and soon enough, I'd be discussing deepname charts with Ulár. Or maybe I could go to bed for a change, try to forget the folly of falling for someone I wanted more than they wanted me. In my mind, the connection to my star was becoming more and more agitated, a shaken feeling rising up my throat with the ferocity of bile. *Fine, I'll leave. I won't bother you again.*

No. This was not how I'd wanted it to go. This was not what I wanted.

The cat miaowed, and Bird pluck it, this was the same cat, a smug-looking brat of a ginger observing us from atop the gently lit, ivy-draped walls of Lilún's poolside garden.

"Away with you! Scram!" I yelled at it, but stopped just before pushing at it with my deepnames. The cat was, arguably, not to blame. Nor did it scram.

I gripped the edge of the pool. "Can I please heat the plucking water?"

"Sure . . ."

I called on my deepnames, and heated the plucking water. The Royal House centered me. At least something was still reliable.

I said, "Look, the whole beautiful people thing, it's . . . it's . . . let me explain. I was ugly as a child. I still am."

Erígra protested, but I ignored them. "I was ugly as a child, and the other kids teased me. They followed my lead, sure, in games and such, but they teased me about my nose . . ." I touched the bridge of my nose.

"What's wrong with your nose?" Erígra looked taken aback.

It wouldn't have hurt as much if my mother hadn't said it all, first. Not the mountain—my human mother. And I believed her, too. I told the other kids myself about the big nose and those other things. They wouldn't have teased me otherwise, or maybe they would've, but with time I came to believe that my mother's words, coming out of my mouth, set it off.

I closed my eyes said, in her exact tone of voice, "My nose looks like a big red candlebulb."

"No!" Lilún exclaimed. "Absolutely not. This doesn't even make sense—and you have more than one brow—and even if you didn't—"

I would not cry. I would not cry.

I remembered how all this had built and built and built, my mother's words growing harsher the older and more rebellious I grew. Conversations and whispers began about my mother and me, and how the healer-keepers would come any day now for both of us, and then they finally came. My mother had said that I was the one who was broken, who was at fault in all this, but the healer-keepers said I was fine.

I could taste the despair and shame and rage of those days. My first powertaking, when I had defended my mother from the healer-keepers. My second powertaking, when I had defended myself from her. In just two weeks, I had acquired two single-syllables. My mother—my mother only had the one three-syllable deepname, weaker and longer than either of mine, and suddenly I was so much more powerful.

I remembered how that had made me feel. Sharp and in control and angry, so angry. I had wanted more. I had wanted to grasp the Warlord's Triangle, the most powerful and dangerous configuration of the land. Three single-syllables.

With an effort, I unclenched my fists. "So I thought about it. If I took one more deepname, I would hold the Warlord. And I could fix *everything*." Fix my mother, the way the healer-keepers couldn't. I knew her best, after all. And I had the aptitude. That power was within my reach, and then, everybody would do what I wanted. I would fix it all. Nobody would tease me, and nobody would tease each other either. And if they dared, I would make them stop. Just thinking about it made my blood run hot in my veins, my nostrils flare. "You don't like this word, fix."

They said, "I, um. I missed the bit about your powertaking. The first two deepnames. You thought it, but did not say."

I laughed, a short, bitter sound. "You've seen me twice, and you already know me."

"Three times, but one of them you ran away from me."

I thought about smiling, and that in itself was progress. "I held off taking the third deepname. I went up the mountain instead to cool off, and I . . . the mountain is my mother, see. My real mother." I swallowed. Lilún . . . I wanted to tell Lilún, but I was making a mess of it.

They made an encouraging noise to go on.

"So I went up the mountain, and I figured out the truth. The Royal House is a better configuration. One, one, and two-syllables: stable and sheltering like the mountain. It is stronger than every other configuration except the Warlord's Triangle, but unlike the Warlord, it does not *force* people. I didn't want to force my friends. I would get what I wanted, but I would have no friends. And I didn't want to force my mother. I just wanted her to love me."

I swallowed. Continued. "So I took a two-syllable last, and formed the Royal House in my mind. And I started calling people beautiful. Climbed Mother Mountain with me? Beautiful. Had interesting deepname power? Beautiful. Brave, honest, good with your hands? Beautiful." I cherished that memory, the growing sense of understanding as my life began to change. "And every guest in my house is certainly beautiful."

Lilún pushed away from their side of the pool and moved closer. "Of course they all wanted to be beautiful for you."

I wanted to bridge the distance and pull them to me, but I did not move. "All people are beautiful in their own way, Lilún." *Even my mother.* But I didn't want to think about that.

"Then why do you say you are ugly?"

It was my turn to look away. *You don't understand. Everybody else is beautiful.*

"The warm water is nice." Lilún moved closer. Their eyes were full of starlight. "You did not want this to be fleeting?"

I smiled at them, still sad, but no longer on the verge of tears. This was mine. Mine and Lilún's. Not my mother's, not even the mountain's.

"We are only beginning, Lilún. Unless you want me to go."

"Then may I call you by your inner name?"

"What, Kekeri?" Oh, Bird. "It's not my inner name, Lilún, it's a nickname, because I . . . because I talked back. And because I was angry. And sure, my mother came up with that, but all my friends thought it was *hilarious.*" It hurt to breathe. I added, after a moment, "My Bird is not even a crow. If you must know, it's a cormorant. But I will keep the plucking name and if I ever have children, I'll bequeath it to them, because I'm just that obstinate."

"Shh. It's all right." Lilún put their hand on my arm. Their touch was thrilling, dizzying, as if we hadn't done anything yet, as if the night was still new. "I don't want you to go. So maybe we can . . ."

That's when the earthquake hit.

It was so abrupt and so enormous that I didn't grasp it at first. There was a sound, like a huge brass bell. The poolside stones cracked, the stones of the one external wall were going down, dragging vines and nightflowers with them. Lilún screamed. My head was bursting from inside like a ripe melon under the knife, but my deepnames, miraculously, were still within reach, and I drew on them.

Then I jumped out of the pool, forming shapes of light with my power. I stretched the protection of my configuration over Lilún's shaking house. I heard the indignant yelp of a cat and saw the bright orange streak for a moment before it disappeared.

The neighborhood teetered on some precarious edge—beyond the ruined wall, I saw other walls tumbling. I raised my hands to the sky and rotated my configuration as fast as I could. Not enough power. I reached through the Keeper's tether to my star just as the second wave hit, and the connection was sputtering—spinning. Wounded. The air smelled of dust and burning.

This was coming from the star in the first place.

While I spun my defenses, Lilún clambered out of the water and called on the Princely Angle, and I saw its bright and delicate light above Lilún's head. They cried, "Let me help you—"

"How?" I yelled, concentrating so hard on holding my structure over Lilún's house that I thought my jaw would dislocate. "How, help me?"

They yelled back, "When you tied me—my configuration was involved too—"

I had no idea what they wanted, except that I felt a glimmer of something, some recognition—

"Use my power," they screamed. "Hold me! Let me join you!" And somehow, *somehow*, I did.

Our structures intertwined, the deepnames settled against each other, fitting, flaring to an even brighter life. Lilún's smaller brightness fit into mine, supporting it, expanding it. I felt enormous, the construct in my hands no longer a triangle of power—it was a small but potent net that unfolded from my exultant, bewildered mind to shield not just Lilún's house, but the whole neighborhood. The connection with my star felt different for a moment, as if it was taking a breath. Calming down. My whole body from head to toe was strung out and taut like a sail bearing a strong wind. This would hurt, later. The knowledge sat in me, detached and unimportant.

The aftershocks were hitting now, but I would hold, and so I held.

Sometime later—not much later, I gauged—the night settled. Around us, I saw the rubble of Lilún's beautiful courtyard. Torn vines. It could have been much worse. Beyond the ruined walls, people were running and yelling.

The power left me with a warm, sharp gush, and I tottered onto the ground, but almost immediately pushed myself up. My whole plucking body hurt like I had kicked it, but I had no time to dwell on that.

I turned my head this way and that. "Lilún!" There they were, sitting on the rubble by the cracked, besmirched pool. They looked dazed, as if time had stopped for them, which it plucking hadn't. I had to be moving. I had to be in Keeper's House. I had to talk to Ulár, as soon as it was possible, about what had just passed. I was naked, and there was a pile of plucking rubble where I'd left my clothes on the stones.

I crossed the distance to the pool in two strides, and grabbed my lover by the shoulder. They recoiled from the touch as if I'd struck them, but there was no time for negotiations now. I let them go, hissing at myself through clenched teeth. "Apologies." I had to find some plucking patience. "Please, Lilún. We have to get to Keeper's House."

They turned their stricken, haunted eyes to me. "We?"

"Don't you see?" I wanted to shake them, to kiss them. "The structure we formed—the structure we formed! This innovation, *your* innovation—I need to know what it means, for our future, for the star—I felt it calming down when we used it—do you have any clothes I can borrow?"

"Ranra." Their voice suddenly sounded very flat, and they closed their eyes. "Can you please slow down."

I almost yelled at them. *Now?!?! You want me to slow down now? People are probably hurt—we need to be moving—we need to be doing—*

Lilún was not Veruma. I could walk away from them, or I could plucking slow down.

I breathed through my nostrils, casting about for some calm. This was harder than anything. "Yes."

"You want me to come to Keeper's House."

I spoke with what seemed to me an exaggerated slowness. "There is something very dangerous going on, but it responded to what we did together. I've never heard of this before—two configurations—I must consult with Ulár. You met him before—tall, lanky, three earrings in one ear . . ." I stopped. Was this still too fast?

"Do you think people died?" said Lilún in a small voice.

"I don't know yet." I'd know more if I wasn't stuck here—but that wasn't fair to Lilún. I said instead, "We will find out. Try to help. If you're coming."

Lilún seemed to shake themself from their reverie. "We should check the house for clothes."

The house itself seemed mostly undamaged, protected by our net, but inside it, things had toppled over. I was wider and somewhat taller than Lilún, but in the end, we found a pair of pants for me, and an embroidered shirt, intended for some celebration, undamaged and loose-fitting enough, and a pair of too-narrow shoes. I was impatient to be going, but the warmth and the feel of Lilún's festival clothing against my skin brought some of the earlier feeling back. "Lover," I said. "Do you want—"

They came to me, wordlessly, and we sighed against each other, faces and limbs pressed together in the darkness. Lilún felt shaken against me, and I hugged them to me fiercely, breathing in the scent of their hair—ash and primrose, all the unspoken promises. "We'll make this work," I muttered. "We'll make this work, by Bird."

They said, "I want you to meet somebody."

"Right now?" I laughed, it was so sudden. A former lover? Their parents? "Can it wait till the morning? We should make our way to Keeper's House now . . ."

They nodded against my shoulder, and did not argue.

Variation the Third:
AGÁR

I am all the serpents

Lilún

I followed Ranra. What else was there to do? It seemed like lifetimes away that we'd walked through the slumbering city, ages ago that we came together under the protection of an ancient stone wall, to the indignant yowls of the cat—but it had just been hours earlier. I wondered what happened to the cat, and if it was even the same cat on my boundary wall earlier. The wall itself was ruined now, rubble crushing the crescent primrose blossoms I'd planted there so carefully.

The damage was worse beyond my neighborhood. It was night still, but the air was pierced by a thousand tiny, bright globes of magical candlebulbs and regular, fire-lit torches. People, both named strong and magicless, ran out of their houses to check on each other and assess the damage. *My nose is like a candlebulb*, she'd said. It wasn't. It was a lovely nose, in fact, perhaps a bit large, but not in a bad way. Ranra's face was expressive, significant, full of life and power, and I wished . . . I wished I could have told this to her before this had happened.

I wanted to slow down, but everything buzzed—the shouts of people and birds, the creaking trees, somewhere the rumble of falling stone. The earth still reverberated under my feet, exuding a kind of heat, an agitation; the air was ripe with dust. Ranra's hand clasping mine felt impatient, her stride assured and all too fast for my stumbling steps. She walked toward Keeper's House, stopping to check in on the wounded and offer magical help. I did my best to assist her, but as this went on, I became more and more disoriented.

I wanted to sit down. I needed to think about every-thing that had happened—the poetry reading, her words, her touches, and how she'd led me, and how good it'd felt to melt into that, how good it was to trust, to be constrained, admired, lavished with her regard and ravished by her; and later how precious it was to share her story of hurt, and how much I wanted to believe her when she said that she did not want this to be fleeting, and how I wasn't sure I believed that yet. And how I wanted to sink even deeper into the feeling of being with Ranra, and how I wasn't ready for a gigantic booming noise that still reverberated in my ears, and how I ended up throwing my magical structure up to join hers, and how true and important it'd felt, for that bright, brief moment, to contribute a part of that structure. And then, how quickly she moved, and moved, and moved, and moved, and I had to stop somewhere.

I sat.

Ranra's arm was yanked by my motion, but she did not let me go. She stopped. Leaned over me, then crouched by me. "Lilún, love, are you all right?"

It was . . . such a not-Ranra thing to say, it almost made me laugh. "You don't have to talk like that to me, Ranra, I am neither sick nor very young."

She barked a laugh. "Yes? I care about you, and you just collapsed on the plucking street. What's left of it, anyway."

I still wasn't looking at her, and that helped. "Give me a moment."

I tugged my hand out of hers, and she stood watch over me as I stared at some bits of stone and dust on the ground. I began rocking back and forth.

Dimly, as if through a veil, I heard people coming and going. I heard Ranra's voice somewhere above me: *No, they're not hurt. No, we don't need assistance, thank you. Do you need assistance?*

My world narrowed to a single piece of stone in front of me. It was reddish-gray and a bit jagged, and it fit nicely in the palm of my hand. It felt dusty to the touch, not unpleasant, but not what I was expecting. I would have dropped it, if not for the ridge of it pressing on my palm, a refreshing sensation that made me think of cold water, made me want to feel wetness on my hands.

Touching the stone reminded me that I had a brass token somewhere. My zúr turtle. I patted my pockets. No, the clothes were new. I had not unbraided my hair, but the turtle fell earlier, in the tavern. It was in the pocket of my other trousers, the ones that were still in the courtyard, covered in rubble.

The loss of the zúr turtle felt jolting, bitter; and strangely enough, that focused me back in my body.

I tucked the stone into my pocket and stood up, not looking at Ranra. "I will follow you, but I cannot look or touch right now."

"Yes," she said. "Are you all right?"

I shrugged. "I need to ruminate on things. When something happens, I go home to think about it. I write a poem. I go out to a gathering place to read the poem. People tell me what they think. I come back home and ruminate on that. I write some more, change things. In the mornings, I go to the grove. I tend to the quince trees, who don't talk to me or tug at me." I did not mention Semberí.

"I'm sorry," Ranra said.

I looked up at her. I expected to see impatience, or annoyance, or anger, but primarily she looked concerned.

"What are you sorry for?" I asked.

"For . . . invading your world."

"But I want you to be in my world." I didn't remember if I'd said this to anybody else before her. Maybe. Probably not. Would she run? If she ran now, would I be relieved? Sad? Relieved and sad?

No relief was forthcoming, because she still waited for me.

I said again, "I want you to be in my world, and I want to . . . to talk, and I want—things not to be exploding." It came out weak and petulant, as if it was her fault that things exploded. "I just want us to have time, Ranra . . ."

"I cannot undo the earthquake, Lilún. It happened, and unless we act, it will keep happening. This is why I thought . . . This is why I said, this is why . . . I thought we had time, Lilún, the pattern seemed to be building slowly, but this—this was not that. I need to act, Lilún, I need to ask Ulár, I need to make a new plan. I want you with me, but I want you to *want* to come with me, Lilún . . ."

I touched the stone in my pocket, its dusty feel discomfiting until I found that sharp, jagged edge again. I hated the stone. I wanted to go back home and look for my turtle. I wanted to sit at my desk and stare at nothing for a while. Perhaps write a poem. I wanted to make Ranra understand all this, but I couldn't, because she was right. It happened, and I had choices to make.

I dropped the stone back onto the ground. Ranra saw, but said nothing.

I said, "I will follow you, but on my own. Just go, and . . . just don't look back, don't wait for me."

She nodded, and began to walk, briskly and with stiff shoulders, through the rubble-strewn streets of Gelle-Geu. She did not stop anymore. She did not look back. I wondered if she thought I would simply go home, but I focused on her figure some distance in front of me. She was moving stiffly in my too-small shoes, and I mimicked her motions without looking at anything else. The roads were blocked with people and debris, and it was a long slog to Keeper's House.

By the time we got to Keeper's House, I was scarcely noticing anything beyond the rhythm of Ranra's movement and the clogging smell of dust in the air, but Keeper's House was brightly lit and mostly undamaged. Ranra brushed aside the questions from the people who rushed to welcome her, and immediately began to give orders.

"Get Ulár, Veruma, Somay, Dorod, Penár, everybody else on my crew you can find, get them into the council chamber, get the Birdforsaken charts in there . . ."—she looked back and saw me, and her face split into a smile. She turned again to her people—" . . . some food and juice. And bring me a pair of shoes and a plucking korob. A clean one." Then she looked at me again, and I wondered if her head ever hurt and if she ever made herself dizzy, but she did not seem dizzy. She asked me, "Is it good to touch you yet? I want to take your hand."

"Yes . . ."

She took my hand and led me into Keeper's House, brushing aside more people. Ranra said to the others, "I'm unharmed and I already asked for the things I need, go get my crew." We walked through a chain of grand rooms until we reached the council chamber with its malachite columns and its central table of polished wood. There were some people there, but I did not look closely.

"Get a chair," Ranra ordered someone. "Not this one, that one. Lilún needs to sit."

I sat in the chair, without noticing much about its shape, size, or color, but it was comfortable. Gingerly, I stretched out my legs.

Ranra leaned over me. "Does it help to sit?"

"Yes, thank you . . ."

She thrust a glass of juice into my hand. "Try to rest

while the people get gathered." Then she darted off somewhere.

The glass in my hand was cold, and I took a sip. A mix of etrog and globe citrus, it was fragrant and sweet with a bitter undertone, lovely and bracing. The world felt clearer now, but I did not move.

Next year, Semberí had said. *We still have time*, Ranra said. My head was pounding.

People were coming in, taking seats at the polished table. A tall man, lanky and long-haired, leaned over the table and thrust his hand at me. "We weren't properly introduced the first time. I am Ulár Viyann."

I did not remember him at all, but I shook his hand. "Erígra Lilún." I thought he would say more, but he seemed content.

Now that I was situated and with some of this lovely juice in me, I began to think, and my thoughts took a predictable turn. I was composing a poem, but not, as I expected, for Ranra.

> *I am not the leader this hour demands.*
> *I am not any leader, Semberí. Will you listen,*
> *you, who shies away from people to haunt the grove*
> *where nobody else comes?*
> *You said we had a year.*

Lines floated in the dimness of my mind and winked out. New ones arose as if from a dream, unpolished, listless, with no embellishment to them.

> *In a single hour the city ashed over.*

> *She jumped up, a structure of salt and gold between*
> *her arms,*
> *unhesitating, and even though I joined,*
> *I couldn't have started this, but you thought I needed*
> *to lead, to command—you should have seen*
> *the speed with which she moves—I could not do this*
> *even if I had ten years, Semberí*

It was clumsy, and maybe not even a poem. I wanted my house back, and my notebook, and my pen, so that I could write this feeling out and excise it, and then either repair the poem or destroy it, but I was paperless, and here, and I wasn't even sure if it mattered.

> *Listen, when it struck, I heard voices inside me,*
> *a whole city of them, each person's flesh around the*
> *same star*
> *and all of them screamed*

"Erígra?" somebody said.

> *we revel*
> *in the complexity of spun towers, our magics, our*
> *mastery—*
> *skimmed foam upon the abyss*

"Erígra!"

I opened my eyes, and the lines that rustled in my ears began to recede. The councilors were here, faces serious and tired, old and young. Ranra was here, too, and Ulár Viyann, and Veruma, and Dorod—I was glad to see Dorod. I was introduced to others—Somay, Penár, Bodavar, and other people whose names and faces I immediately struggled to remember.

Ranra spread some charts on the table. Deepname charts of the Sputtering Star, with a dense core of single-syllables at the center of the star, and the tender, long tendrils of weaker four- and five-syllable deepnames at the very edges.

"Now that we are gathered," Ranra said, "the strongest and wisest of us, the three-named strong . . ."

Except for Erígra Lilún, I waited for her to say, but she went on.

" . . . I call upon us to take council. The future we feared is coming to pass, and months ahead of our most dire predictions. For the record, I thought we had a plucking year at least, and all of you said so."

Ulár spoke. "Veruma Soli and Erígra Lilún are both two-named strong. Yet they are here, and it is clear why they both are here."

Ranra leaned over, her face too close to Ulár's. "You mean to imply that I drag all my lovers here? We would need more chairs if I did. And probably a bigger room."

Ulár shrugged. Veruma crossed her arms at her chest, her expression sour.

Ranra cleared her throat. "Look, Veruma has always been a part of our councils. As for Erígra Lilún, they have the potential of a three-named strong, moreover, the potential of a starkeeper. Erígra belongs here."

"We are all failed starkeepers here," Somay said. "I mean, except you, Ranra, an actual starkeeper." Somay was an ichidi, fiftyish, short, and frustrated-looking.

An abstract ichar token dangled from their ear. "Every one of us here, at least every three-named strong, has that potential."

"My goal is not to exclude anyone," Ulár chimed in. "I'm asking for accuracy. I'm asking for greater accuracy from myself, too, since Ranra thinks my charts are off by a year."

I was fascinated despite myself, by this person Ulár, and by Ranra's earlier praise of him. She liked people who pushed back. Had she called Ulár beautiful, after the arguments? I giggled, and everybody stared at me. I felt blood rising to my cheeks.

I said, "I have no potential to be a starkeeper." I should have told this more explicitly to Semberí, but I did not understand this clearly myself before. I did now. "I am not the leader this hour demands. I am not a leader at all. I tend to the quince trees on a hill by the sea, and I write poems, that's all."

Ranra still faced Ulár. "When the event occurred, I called on my deepnames to try to hold the area safe. Erígra formed their own structure, and joined me. I have no idea what they did, but I could use the power generated from *two* configurations, and when I harnessed it, I protected the whole Bird-pecked neighborhood. My connection with the star itself felt altered by this. It felt calmer. We *must* have Erígra, this is *their* innovation, probably the most important innovation of our plucking lives, and we *must* develop this further, we *must* use it to fix this. Mend this. Heal."

Ulár tore his gaze away from Ranra's, and spoke to me. "Is this true?"

"Yes," I said.

"Can you demonstrate this?"

"I have no idea." I was not going to lead these people, but neither was I going to sit idle and let Ranra carry everything alone while her advisors only pushed back. "But I'm certainly willing to try."

I closed my eyes and spoke my deepnames in my mind. Here in the quiet room with everybody watching, the snap-like explosion in my mind was even more pronounced. At least the pain did not last. My deepnames flared to life—two beacons of light—and I spun and combined them like I remembered doing before. Ranra, too, engaged her configuration. I looked at her. She was so striking, so focused, anger and will and hope condensed in a fist.

I reached out to her with my construct, and she moved her own structure closer, but absolutely nothing happened. We both, as on cue, spun our constructs above the expanse of the table, but the lines of light remained distinct.

I gave up at last, feeling self-conscious and small under the weight of so many glances. I folded my deepnames back into my mind. "Maybe we cannot replicate it."

"We will," Ranra said. Her configuration was still engaged. "Think back, Lilún—to the moment—what you felt, what I did . . ."

"You constructed a triangle. Held it over your head—"

As I spoke, Ranra thrust her arms up like she'd done before. Her configuration rotated faster and faster,

121

creating brilliant, overlapping triangles of light. Her face looked enraptured, exultant, and I wanted, I wanted to help her, to be a part of this, a part of her. I no longer thought about people who watched us. My world narrowed down on Ranra, on her outthrust arms, and my deepnames flared to life again. I felt no pain as I spun the Princely Angle toward Ranra's construct, and our structures rotated and wound against each other. Joining. I felt my own power being lifted from me, but still firmly rooted in my mind as Ranra took hold of it. The net between her arms expanded, shimmering, whispering, filling the room with cold burning.

"Hold it!" Ulár yelled. "Hold it right there!" He was scribbling furiously on a piece of paper in front of him, but he didn't look down—his eyes were focused on the construct we made. At least two others seemed to be taking notes. The rest of them just gaped at us. The act of noticing other people broke my concentration, and the blended configuration we'd made unraveled.

"Yes!!!" shouted Ranra, who still held on to her now-diminished power. "You see. You see!"

"I have to try this." Ulár's voice trembled with excitement. He engaged his own magic. It was a Builder's Triangle of one, two, and three syllables, a precise and stable configuration that lent itself easily to scholarly endeavors. He spun his construct toward Ranra. But no matter how hard they tried to fling their magics together, the two configurations circled each other like vultures, never actually combining.

Long minutes passed. Finally, both Ranra and Ulár dropped their magics and sat down.

"Perhaps you are right," Ranra said, "that we need to be lovers."

"All of us?" said Ulár. "That wasn't what I was thinking." Then, gruffly, he said, "If it's so, that's too bad. I'm adar."

"I'm sorry about . . ." Ranra said. "I meant no disrespect, and we will try to find . . ."

Ulár said, "Shh."

An awkward silence fell, interrupted only by the sound of Ulár's pen scribbling.

Eventually he looked up. "I actually think this can be replicated without the need for an extremely large childless gathering. And if we can't, there's the two of you."

Ranra said, "Two is not enough. We need a crowd."

"Yes, I got that," said Ulár.

"And then what?" said Somay. "Provided this is doable, as Ulár says—you want to combine the power of this crowd and take control of it, all of our magics at your command—that must be your plan—"

"It is," Ranra said.

"So we entrust you with all our magic. And then what?" Somay asked.

"Then," said Ranra, "I heal."

She was beautiful to look at, Ranra, in that terrible way that a storm is beautiful, full of brilliance and rage, reaching higher and higher into the sky. "I will heal the star from its nightmares. Earthquakes will cease. The star will wake up, and I will ask for its consent. I will bond with it, properly this time, and then I will act as its keeper according to the ancient laws of starlore and the *Starkeeper's Primer*."

Everybody in the room just stared at her.

Ranra laughed. "Don't stare at me as if I've suddenly sprouted the Warlord's Triangle. If the star doesn't want me when it wakes, I will step down, gladly. After this is done."

"And what if we cannot replicate this with a crowd?" said Ulár.

"Then we try again, until we can, or until someone comes up with a better idea." Ranra looked around the room, challenge in her gaze. "Keeper Terein gave up. We all watched him for years as his despair deepened. We were unwilling to demote him, we wanted to be compassionate and do everything according to tradition—and we all thought we had more time, five years, a year—but it doesn't seem like we have the time. The star is suffering now and needs our aid now. I will not despair until I have done the work. And I cannot do it alone. This will take all of us."

Veruma, who had been silent through the whole council, spoke now. "Like good healer-keepers?"

The change in Ranra's mood was palpable. "How dare you," she hissed, and I recoiled from her anger, her clenched fists, even though I had no idea what Veruma implied. "You have a better solution? Sit in a corner, unwilling to look at a chart, hoping that someone else will finish the story we abandon?"

"Not every story has a good end," Veruma said, stubborn. "What if you cannot heal the star?"

With a visible effort, Ranra unclenched her fists. Exhaled. "I have formed the structure twice now, Veruma. The star responded to me like never before. We *must* attempt this." Ranra looked around the room. "We will work to replicate and expand on Erígra's discovery, and then we will come together. What do you say, Dorod?"

The shipwright, who had been silent throughout the meeting, now smiled benignly. "An interesting idea, for sure. I like how it sprung fully fledged from your mind."

"You too think it's hopeless," said Ranra. "You think I am a child and do not understand the dangers of this path. I do. I believe we must take this risk, and I ask you to join me. I hope every three-named strong says yes, but especially you."

"You are the leader of this hour," Dorod said. "I respect you and I respect your choice, but I don't think this endeavor is for me—my apologies. I am going to keep building and outfitting my ships."

"We don't need more ships, Dorod." Ranra frowned. "We need unity."

"You are the starkeeper and I am a shipwright," said Dorod. "From where I stand, we definitely need more ships."

The council broke up after this, with people talking to each other, and to Ranra. She stood, glowering, defiant, in the center of them. It would have been useless to talk to her. I sat in my chair just resting, taking in the room—the soaring coved ceiling painted blue, with the map of the stars gilt-traced on it, the chiseled malachite columns. Ranra wore an emerald green korob. My festival shirt poked from underneath it.

Across the polished expanse of the table, Ulár winked

at me. His hair wasn't braided today—perhaps he'd been woken up by the earthquake. He said, "They will think about it for an hour or two and come around. This is the best idea of the generation."

I gulped. "I thought you were opposed?"

"Only the gatherings bit. People who are not adar always want their parties, no matter what's going on. But the actual substance of this?" Ulár grinned, and at that moment I saw him as a young boy clutching a model of deepname structures made from sticks. "How can I be against new magic, Erígra? That's all I want from life. It's the best."

He produced a hair tie from his pocket and bound his long, frizzy hair into a loose knot. "If you don't mind, let's talk about what happened when you combined your configuration with Ranra's—I believe the construct's origin was yours, not hers . . ."

I said, "She was the first to draw on her deepnames."

"Sure, but you were the one who connected."

I smiled back at him, hesitantly. His words made me feel seen. "Yes, I offered my magic, and sent my structure to hers. She found a way to embrace it."

"Excellent," said Ulár. "We'll start from you as the originator . . . I want to know about the exact sensations you felt—you said her deepnames were already engaged?" He flitted from question to question, jotting notes as I attempted to remember.

I hoped to get sleep at some point, and then to take Ranra to see Semberí, but it would be hours yet before we took a break.

Ranra

I woke up in bed next to the sleeping Lilún. The bed, thank Bird, was new—lower and firmer than the old one, and most importantly, mine. Lilún and I had had no chance for anything last night—they were exhausted by work and overwhelmed by the strangeness of staying at Keeper's House. I had hugged them to sleep. Now, with the light climbing through the shuttered window, they looked peaceful and so heartbreakingly beautiful in their trust that for a moment I had to remind myself that this was real. Like me, Veruma had been early to rise, and always in a foul mood; but Lilún only nestled deeper into the cushions. They had wanted to introduce me to someone—insisted, even—but it wasn't happening right now.

I tiptoed out of the bedroom, got dressed, and conferred with my people in one of the nearby chambers where Terein used to have breakfast. It was hexagonal and airy, with an inlaid mosaic floor depicting sea serpents and fanciful fish, and not much furniture except for a few couches covered in summer white.

A single large window overlooked the city, and I got my first good look at it after the earthquake. The magical defenses at Keeper's House had held. We suffered no damage, not even a fallen bookshelf in the library. The rest of the city was not so lucky. Gelle-Geu, a city of some twenty thousand, lay wounded before my eyes. I saw caved-in roofs and scattered rubble. Farther west,

Lilún's neighborhood was the best preserved of them all, so different from the others that I could easily detect it. Above the stricken city the Mother Mountain towered, her peak drowned in gray clouds.

More people were coming into the room, but not every councilor was present. Somay and Bodavar were already out, helping our people. Dorod, I assumed, was with the ships. Penár made sure that I had breakfast rollups and tea, but she, too, was eager to leave. Veruma was nowhere to be seen, and just as I was about to ask after her, Ulár edged into the room, carrying an armful of scrolls. I doubted he'd slept at all. His red-rimmed eyes shone with a feverish light.

He said, "You were right. We don't have a year. Look."

He had redrawn the charts completely, sometime before dawn. The scrolls were criss-crossed with thin, agitated lines, connecting with what felt like thousands of singular strands of four and five-syllable deepname tendrils jutting out of the star like a terrified person's hair standing on end.

"What am I looking at?" I asked.

"I have no idea, Ranra, to tell you the truth. Nothing good."

"Well, you tell me, Ulár, you charted this . . ."

He slapped another chart on top of the first. The deepname chains—the hairs of long deepnames I saw in the first chart—looked detached on this chart, disconnected from the star. Hair torn out?

"This was charted with a five-hour interval," Ulár explained. "I worked without pause, on my own—after I was done working with Erígra, and only because they collapsed. No, don't look at me like that, I did not make them collapse, they were exhausted. This—look here—"

He pointed at the first chart. "As I explained before, when agitation occurs, long deepnames are extruded out of the core of the dense, one-syllable and two-syllable deepnames that make the center of the star. The star, essentially, expands—there is more deepname length, but less stability. These deepnames are weak and unstable, and suddenly there is more star and the land is too close. This causes agitation to the land. An earthquake. The star then contracts."

He moved to the second chart. "During contraction, the long deepname chains are torn out. This causes aftershocks, which travel all the way to the core of the star, making it even more agitated. Long deepnames begin to be extruded again. This pattern then repeats, faster and stronger than before."

I said, "Like a person who's disturbed and can't calm down."

Ulár frowned. "Like a big ball of deepnames which has become unbalanced for unknown reasons, and has entered an escalating pattern of unbalancing."

"Ulár. Please." But he was literal, and there was little I could or should do about that.

"How much time do you think we have?"

"I don't know," he said. "Perhaps it will calm down on its own, but if it doesn't, not a year. A few months if we're lucky."

"And then?"

I heard a mewling sound, and looked up from the chart to see Veruma carrying in the ginger. The cat looked indignant and worse for wear, dusty and disheveled, but the swirl on their side was still discernible, and made me smile.

"Long time no see," I said, primarily to the cat. Veruma was not in my good graces at the moment. Her remark about the healer-keepers still stung. It was about my mother, and I had postponed thinking about it, but now seeing Veruma, I was reminded.

She said, "Good morning, Ranra. Um, I found . . ."

Ulár tugged my sleeve, getting my attention back to the charts. "And then, during the expansion phases, the star will be too large and will push the isles, disturbing or heating them. During contraction, the sea will rush in."

"It's not that bad." Veruma joined us at the breakfast table, where Ulár's charts were spread. She grabbed an egg pocket and shoved it into her mouth. The cat clawed at her chest, and she absentmindedly grabbed another pocket, tore it in half and fed him. "The city is shaken, not destroyed. Our people are working. Our losses of life are minor. And, by Bird, you all should stop moping and keep working on that method of yours that a mere two-named strong like me cannot encompass, and *fix this*."

I should have said all this myself. These should have been my words. She used my tone, even. Was she saying this to spite me? Shame me?

I snapped, "Yes, yes, Veruma, just like good healer-keepers. You mentioned yesterday."

Blood rushed to her cheeks, and she had the grace to look down. "I'm sorry, Ranra. I really shouldn't have said that."

"No, you shouldn't have." But it made me feel better that she apologized.

I stretched out my hand, and the cat allowed himself to be petted, purring softly under my fingers. "Does he have a name? Has anybody found his person?"

"I asked around; many people are visited by this cat, but he doesn't seem to have a person. Or a name. Most people agree that our cat is a he, though not all."

"Hmmm . . ." I had no idea whether cats had gatherings and ceremonies of their own, or opinions about human language forms. but then, cats were inscrutable. We could come up with a name, at least. "Stray?" I said. "Swirly? Egg pocket?"

The cat hissed at me for daring to suggest such silly names.

"Gogor," said Ulár, not lifting his eyes off the chart.

The cat twisted out of Veruma's hands, jumped to the floor and trotted toward the exit, clearly done with our strange ideas. We all looked after him, but none of us pursued him, and the room lost some of its light.

"I need to be moving," I said. "Ulár, please continue— that is, you need to sleep—"

"I'll be fine," he said. "Don't get me wrong, sleep is nice and everything . . ."

I left him to his own devices. Veruma tagged along with me as I made rounds of the city, offering magical power and my reassurances to the shaken but undaunted islanders. I could see how Veruma got her good cheer, but Ulár's words rang in my ears. Perhaps this would go away on its own, but if not . . . Perhaps there was no reason to rebuild.

No. I would make it work. We would make it work. Somay and some of our best Strong Builders were working with the townspeople now. Gelle-Geu was beautiful to me—its broken towers and unbroken spirit, its intricacy, its learning, its carefree and passionate ways. We would survive this and rebuild. Before the year was out. I'd see to it.

As we walked through the city, Veruma and I didn't say much to each other, and it was incredibly awkward. I had no idea why she wanted to come with me, but her being here kept reminding me of her words, and of the reason for her words, and the fact that I kept delaying. At last I gave up. "I'm going to see my mother. You can come if you want, or not."

She squeezed my shoulder. "I'll come, of course. You're doing the right thing . . ."

"I don't want to talk about it." I turned away from Veruma and strode through the streets toward my mother's house, in the raingardens' neighborhood in the southern part of the city. The houses here, built on solid grids of deepnames and reinforced with layers of potent magic, survived the earthquake mostly intact, with damaged roofs and torn doors. My steps grew heavier as I approached, and my ears filled with noise. *Nose too big—only one brow—who would want to be your friend—trusting your silly little friends more than your own mother—you think deepnames are everything, but I know the truth of you—*

My mother's house was small, made of stone, covered thickly in flowering vines. She sat in the small, shaded front yard, her hands on the potter's wheel, turning and turning a raw clay pot. A neighbor sat on the stone stair, and another on a stoop, to keep her company. Neither the house nor my mother seemed damaged.

She lifted her eyes up at me and scowled. "Took you long enough to show any care at all about your mother's life."

I felt the old feelings flare in me: resentment, anger, helplessness at the sight of her. I bit my lip. Anything I could say would not make this well. *Last we spoke, you said you didn't want to come to my ascension revels. Did you think I was too ugly to celebrate?*

"Adira, please," said the neighbor who sat on the chair. "She came to see you. Please be gentle."

"Do you want me to lie? I merely speak my mind." My mother's hands, wrinkled now, moved of their own accord, shaping a perfect, thin-walled pot. "What will you do to me? Call the healer-keepers at me again? Oh, please stop saving people's lives and come right away, old Adira said something we didn't like!"

"She was perfectly fine earlier this morning," said the neighbor on the stoop. "It's nice of you to come."

My mother's head turned from one woman to another. "You'd think with how much she crowed about the old Keeper, she'd have everything sorted in a day, but here we go. An earthquake. Job wasn't so easy after all. Job's not even real—how can you *keep* the star? Prevent earthquakes? Pfah! I told her to find a job that made sense, but she never had what it takes."

"Shh, dear," said the neighbor in the chair. "Ranra just wants to check in on you."

I still hadn't said a word. The problem with the things

my mother said was that everybody was used to her. Healer-keepers had intervened when I was fifteen, but nobody wanted to do anything since then. Deep illnesses of the mind were subtle in most of their forms, untreatable even by the healer-keepers; the best we could do is keep an eye on people who were not well. Now that my mother lived on her own and did not need to take care of a child, the things she said were seen as quirks, something that did not need intervention. But I remembered living here, remembered her words and her threats and occasional violence. She always said I was a failure, and she said it still. Sometimes, I still believed her.

"Goodbye," I said.

"Sure." My mother's hands moved deftly, shaping a neck for the vessel, thinner and thinner and taller and taller. It had no purpose and could soon collapse into itself, but my mother would make it look beautiful.

"It was nice of you to come, anyway," said the neighbor on the stoop. The other nodded vigorously.

Veruma dragged me away, and I still hadn't said anything. Once we were out of sight, Veruma put her hand on my shoulder. "She doesn't mean any of it."

"How do you know?" I said, a lump in my throat. "She always says those things. I always disappoint her." *And I cannot fix her. And you think that's why I want to fix the star.*

"She's ill," Veruma said. "Have some compassion— she cannot do anything about this—"

"She doesn't want to," I snapped. "If she wanted to, there would be hope—but she thinks she's fine and right."

"Adira is not well, but at least she's stable." Veruma said in a soothing tone. "I'm sorry . . ."

"Everybody always protected her. What about me?" But that wasn't even true. The healer-keepers were called because of me. It was so much easier to mend broken bones than treat the many ailments of the mind; the healer-keepers could not *fix* my mother, nor did she consent to be treated so. But they could separate us. I was given a house and support to live on my own, with teachers and friends and the families of my friends who visited and helped me. The healer-keepers came to check on me, and taught me how to calm my anger by breathing. I turned out fine.

"You are strong. You took care of yourself," said Veruma. "I'm sorry I said what I said earlier, it was cruel of me . . ."

"You already apologized." I said gruffly. "The star is nothing like my mother. I'm not responsible for my mother, but I am responsible for the star. We can do this. We can heal the star together." I had been so certain earlier, but now my mouth felt bitter.

"I trust you," said Veruma, and that made me feel even worse.

Lilún

Ranra was gone when I woke up, groggy and disoriented, in her bed. The light creeping through the blinds was bright; it had to have been at least mid-morning.

Hours later than my usual, except that I rose late those days, it seemed. With thoughts came memories, flooding me with the ash and bitterness of yesterday's earthquake. I had to check on Semberí.

Shaking fatigue from my stiff limbs, I dressed and left in search of Ulár. I had promised him to continue our work—but he, too, had succumbed to slumber, sprawled like a tall, skinny cat on a rigid, carved couch in one of the side rooms. A real cat—the familiar ginger—sprawled by his side.

"Ulár?" I whispered.

He waved his hand in the general direction of the cat and muttered, "Go away, Gogor," without opening his eyes. The cat yawned with a deliberate slowness, but did not otherwise move.

I stole a pastry from the refreshment tray on the side table and snuck out, wiping my hand on my pants. People seemed scarce in Keeper's House, and I made my escape without too many conversations. Outside, the late spring sun shone crisp and bright. Named strong and magicless people alike milled in the streets, clearing stones and debris, cheering each other on with songs and offers of honeyed dough pockets and quince wine. The named strong called on their magic to move the rubble, and someone released a deepname firework of a large, silvery dancing dragon that snapped around at clouds. This was a work of a three-named strong—two of them, to be precise—I spotted a second firework, a long sea serpent of deepname light, that was making circles in the air farther west. Somay and, if I wasn't mistaken, Bodavar. My spirits lifted despite myself, but

I hoped this wouldn't turn into a spontaneous party, and I felt a bit guilty to have escaped Ulár.

Semberí's hill was open to me, but the sea lapped against the rocks here with a particular vehemence. From far above me on the hill, I could hear a plaintive, desolate voice singing. I sped up, trying to catch the words.

> *I carried a piece*
> *of rotten fruit when I walked on water*
> *my hands were occupied*
> *my mouth was full of murmuring the wave*

The voice faded, as if the singer was walking away; but the lilt of it, the ancient pronunciations, were unmistakable. Semberí—I had no idea they could sing—could a ghost even sing? My blood thumping in my ears, I ran up, catching a glimpse of the song, then losing it again.

> *The star I cradled kept me fed*
> *I lost my death as I walked on water*
> *I lost it all except the rotten fruit*

At last I emerged in the grove and stopped myself, panting and bent with my hands on my knees, in front of Semberí. I had no idea why they sang, or what, and I wanted to know, and I wanted to compliment them, but for now, I was wheezing. When I managed to straighten at last, my ancestor's visage was ice-cold, as if every tatter of their ghostly garment was frozen— but the hole of their mouth moved, shaping their song again.

The grove that grew a thousand years
and never knew my death—

They clamped their mouth shut—or rather, their mouth just dissolved in the white film of their face, so that for a long moment they were mouthless.

"I didn't know you could sing." This was about the last thing I should have said, but I just blurted it. Talking to people was never my strength, not even to my own ancestor.

Semberí's face formed a new mouth, round and overly large. Within it, darkness gaped. They ignored my clumsy question. "The grove that grew a thousand years. That scans better than nine hundred and ninety-nine years, doesn't it, Erígra?"

Semberí liked to speak in riddles, but I thought I could begin to unravel this one, and it made me cold all over. "What happened?" I asked, already guessing the answer. "What happened, nine hundred and ninety-nine years ago?"

"You know the answer." Semberí said, cold.

"The Birdcoming," I whispered.

"Yes, the Birdcoming. It's been ninety-nine years and nine hundred more since my star hung, suspended, motionless, waiting its turn by the side of its restless dark sibling the Orphan, Star of Despair, waiting for the Starcounter and Ladder to finish their courting." Semberí looked angry, and hurt.

"In a year, on the anniversary of the Birdcoming, the star will remember its worst day, the endless dance, the churning closeness of the Orphan Star by its side. It will remember all and despair. It is remembering it even now—in the throes of nightmares," said Semberí. "You must attend to the star and learn how to heal it."

"Not me, Semberí. Ranra said she would heal the star, if we all . . ."

"Ranra, Ranra!" The tone Semberí took was mocking. "She is no healer. Has she even read a book about healing? Tended to a tree? This needs a gentle touch. The work needs someone patient, slow-growing, to figure this out after almost a thousand years, before the anniversary . . ."

I had heard or sensed this before, in my reverie on this very hill, in the words of my poem. I pushed it aside. Semberí disliked Ranra for some reason, and Ranra was the one leading us. "She has a plan. It's a good one, and we'll all take a part in it—let me bring her to you," I pleaded. "Talk to her, see what you think for yourself when you hear the plan."

"Pfah." And with the sound of a popping bubble, they dissipated.

I stood there, glaring what I hoped was after them, even though I had no idea which direction they had gone.

"Semberí," I shouted at last. "Semberí! Let her come back here with me."

There was no response, but in a while, the nearest trees moved their limbs together, as if moved by an unseen wind. A disembodied voice hissed, *I'll be around.*

Ranra

After the earthquake, I saw my lover only at night. I wanted more than the nights. I wanted all time to be ours, to sink into our newness. Mornings to wander up the mountain and get lost there, among the boulders and pines. Days to listen to Lilún's poetry, evenings to take them sailing. But all we had was the night. At all other times I was busy with the rebuilding efforts, and Lilún was working with Ulár to discover the geometry of our unity.

On the fourth day, they made progress. Two different people with two deepnames of equal lengths could connect together if they practiced. The mechanics were convoluted, but the participants did not need to be lovers, just closely familiar. That was a relief—for all Ulár joked about non-adar people's fondness for gatherings, few of us would want a childless gathering to become a source of this work.

It was our people's weakest, longest deepnames which formed the connection. The two-syllable in my Royal House first locked with the two-syllable in Lilún's Princely Angle—not our stronger, single-syllables. Ulár, whose longest deepname was a three-syllable, hadn't yet managed to form a connection with either of us, but he didn't seem discouraged. He was going to try connecting with Somay next. Penár, too, had a three-syllable in her Builder's Triangle, but I sent her to the outer islands with healers and supplies.

Ulár's eyes were perpetually red, and I wondered if

he had slept at all since the earthquake. I did not care if I slept, myself; I felt energized and impatient, and my people had to chase me to bed.

On the morning of the fifth day after the earthquake, Lilún roused me before dawn, and together we made our way out of Keeper's House. At my lover's urging, I refused guards and followed them, not caring much where we went. Our courtship was so new, the world so fragile, and this was important to Lilún; that alone made me feel fresh and excited, eager for a small adventure away from the devastations of the earthquake.

We left the main streets and headed toward the harbor and then north, up a hill. Even with the damage and debris, the view was captivating—a verdant hill covered in fruit trees, overlooking the sea and the harbor southeast. To the northeast, the snowy peak of Mother Mountain grazed the clouds.

Lilún had been secretive about this. I didn't mind a surprise, but my curiosity got the better of me. "Will we meet your fathers?" I asked them.

"My fathers have retired to Agara Island." Lilún waved vaguely toward the northwest, where a small island housed a community of older men who preferred the company of other men. "I hope they are all right."

"We sent supplies and healers to Agara and Mehmey," I said. "Penár took one of Dorod's tradeships—I'm glad they are good for something."

Lilún nodded and kept walking up the hill. The morning was crisp, the smell of the sea and the grasses was pleasing, the climb stretched the muscles of my calves and made me feel freer and more joyful than I'd been since the earthquake. This was Lilún's place. Birds sang in the quince grove. Many of the trees had lost limbs, but ripening fruit hung on the surviving boughs, and the fragrant, delicate smell of the trees and the earth made me smile. I took Lilún's hand, pulled them to me and kissed them, and they sighed into me at first, but then pushed me away. "Not now, Ranra. We are almost there."

"You are there," somebody said. The new voice was cold and unpleasant, each syllable carefully enunciated. "And I would appreciate it if you did not embrace in my presence. This is not the Birdcoming."

Lilún stepped away from me. I saw the speaker. An apparition of white and blue, tattered and brooding. Their body and face were of whitish smoke. I saw five-braided strands of seafoam around their head, marking them, so I gathered, as ichidi. An abstract agár token formed out of foam and air hung, for a moment, from their wispy braids, then dissolved into whiteness: *I am all the serpents.* All genders—at once or in turn—in one semitransparent form. The ghost's eyes were of sunken gray vapor, and anger was clear in them.

Lilún coughed into their hand. "Allow me to introduce the current starkeeper of the Star of the Tides, Ranra Kekeri . . ."

"I know who she is," said the ghost, with the same tone of slow, cold anger.

"You said you would see her," said Lilún, their tone reproachful.

"I said," the ghost said, "that I would be around. I am always around."

Lilún turned to me. "This is the first starkeeper of the Star of the Tides, my ancestor, Semberí."

Ah. I frowned. Considered the implications. All this time Semberí—if this really was Semberí—was around to share their wisdom, but not, evidently, with me. With Lilún. And Lilún did not tell me.

Except they tried to tell me, and repeatedly. They had been asking me to come with them for days. I just—I had other things to do.

I exhaled, letting go of my anger at Lilún and Semberí both, or at least I made the effort. The ghost glared at me. I had to say something.

Nice to make your acquaintance? But it wasn't. My mother would sometimes look at me with such eyes. *Your visage disappoints me and your existence burdens me.* She rarely spoke it out loud, but often enough that I knew how it felt and what it meant.

Semberí wasn't anybody's *mother*, for Bird's sake. It wasn't right for me to hate them just because they hated me. I had to connect with them somehow. I could start with hello.

I bowed, formally, and straightened. "I greet you, Semberí. I . . ."

The ghost interrupted me with a vehement motion of a semitransparent arm. Spoke to Lilún. "You did not tell me you were lovers, when you asked to bring her here. To *embrace* in *my grove.*"

Lilún's cheeks flushed. This was going all wrong.

"Our relationship is very new," I began to explain. "We did not mean—"

"You have everything. My house. My library. My star.

And now, Erígra, too." Semberí's ghostly body swung violently, as if tossed by a nonexistent wind. "Whatever you want you just grab, whether or not it's yours."

So much for connecting with them. No, they weren't my mother—the insults were all new. "Erígra is their own. I do not *have* them." I crossed my arms at my chest. "At least you don't insult my appearance!"

"What?" Semberí hissed. "What do I care about your appearance? I don't care about you at all. Erígra should have been starkeeper."

I said, "I am the starkeeper now." No, this wasn't like talking to my mother. The ghost made sense, they just didn't like me. And I had no idea if I could make them like me, or if I cared to try. "Erígra is supporting me, they are part of this. All of us are part of this. Many people are doing this work now. None of us can do this work alone. I want to heal the star, Semberí."

Lilún frowned, and I suddenly heard what they heard—how the word *heal* had replaced the word *fix*, which they'd asked me not to use, but the two words fell from my mouth in the same way.

Semberí pounced on my hesitation. "Do you really think *you* can heal the Sputtering Star? Have you healed anyone in your life?"

I looked away. This wasn't a question about my mother. Healing was a specialized profession that focused on people's physical bodies. The fresher the wound, the easier it was to heal, or more accurately to undo, especially if the healer was a three-named strong. Minds were a different matter. Nobody knew what to do with the illnesses of the mind, except for the most acute cases, when calming magics could be administered by healer-keepers for a brief moment before the mind's patterns reasserted themselves.

You cannot fix her, Ranra. Walk away.

But stars didn't have human minds, nor did they have bones that could break and be knit together. My connection with the star was different.

"I have never healed a person," I said, "but the star doesn't have a body of flesh. I've mended plenty—ships damaged by storms, houses shaken by earthquakes—I hold the Royal House, the configuration of generous benevolence . . ."

"I am familiar with the basic configurations," the ghost said. And then, "At least you do not wield the Warlord's Triangle. Bird be praised."

Lilún chuckled. They were standing by a tree, their hand on its slender, gnarled trunk, and I wondered if they were going to speak. But it was Semberí who spoke next. "Do you even know what the twelve stars *are?*"

"Do you think I'm a child, or unfamiliar with starlore?" I did not swear, but it was a close call. "But I'm sure you will tell me."

"Go choke on a beak," said Semberí.

I glared at them, and the ghost glared back, the swirling gray vortices of their eyes pulling at me. At least, Semberí spoke. "The stars are travelers, each from a different world. Did you know that? No? I thought so. Bird had gathered them all in her tail before journeying here. She intended to entrust the stars to us. This we, the first starkeepers, figured out between ourselves."

No, I had no idea. This wasn't in the *Starkeeper's*

Primer, or in Semberí's archives. Perhaps they were lying, but why would they lie?

The ghost continued. "Each star was made from thousands and thousands of deepnames. Each star came from elsewhere. Each star clung to the tail of the goddess as she flew through the abysses which lie between worlds. Figure it out for yourself, starkeeper. What are the twelve stars? Who are the twelve stars? What would it take to heal such a being?"

Semberí's words snared me, drew me in, but I couldn't for the life of me figure out what they wanted me to say. "I am doing my best! If you know something I don't, then teach me."

The ghost swirled in the air again, agitated. "Erígra should have been starkeeper, but they learned nothing, too."

"I did not want to become a starkeeper, Semberí," said Lilún, their voice tired. I wondered how many times they had had this conversation. "I cannot do this work, I cannot do the people thing . . ."

"Bird peck the people thing," sputtered the ghost. "A starkeeper's job is to keep their star safe. It's in the title. But now, of course, she's got you, Erígra—"

"You yourself told me to go see her!"

"I thought you would see how badly she's suited to the task—I thought it would spur you to action, not, not to tangle with her!"

"Semberí, please," said Lilún, their voice placating. "I brought Ranra so she could tell you about our endeavor. I am with her of my own free will. I choose to be. She is doing the work, she is leading our crew. I support her by choice. The islands are in danger. You told me the same thing yourself, Semberí. I brought her here because I'm asking you to help us."

"I helped you already," said the ghost. "You still have almost a year to figure it out."

"Ulár believes it is less than a year," I interjected. "I, too, think so. Much less."

The ghost snarled. "I have no idea who this fool Ulár might be. I said what I said. To heal, you must first understand what hurts. To heal, you must first become trusted."

And then they streamed at me and through me, an icy gust through my flesh, yelling, "And take your courting with you when you go!"

With a vehement lurch, we were thrown out of there, and found ourselves sprawled on the grass at the foot of the hill.

I struggled to my knees, then up. Lilún half-rose, too. Grabbed my wrists. Beyond us, to the north, the quince hill was now shrouded in mist.

I felt angry. So angry. I twisted my wrists out of Lilún's grasp. "What do you want from me? Why did you bring me here?"

"I want you to know that I think Semberí is wrong," they said. "I cannot be starkeeper."

"You keep saying this. But you can. You can take the Royal House right now, and be just as good as I am and better—and Semberí's right, this job is about the star, not endless plucking gatherings . . . The council can tend to the isles, to trade, to everything that requires talking to people."

"Maybe," they said dubiously. "But you are trying to keep the star. You are taking the risks, you are making the decisions, bringing people together . . . steering the council . . . and I admire you for that." They struggled to their feet, their breath shaken, and my anger morphed into a fierce protectiveness and need.

"Lilún—"

"So lead me. I will support you."

I took them by the back of their neck. The motion, instinctive and powerful, was fraught too, so early into our dance; but Lilún's eyes, locked on mine, gave me nothing but passion. I pulled them to me, thinking about Semberí's fierce resistance to our courtship. Well, they'd asked me take it elsewhere, and I was elsewhere enough. The hour was mine, and so was my ichidi, freely given and in mutual desire, and nobody else had the right to tell me what to do.

I kissed Lilún, deeply, ferociously, while mists swirled around the quince hill to the north, and the sea murmured below. Lilún raised their hand, calling the Princely Angle, and I engaged my own configuration. This was becoming practiced. I grasped Lilún's freely shared magic in mine. I felt huge, like I'd grown wings and become Bird, rising into the endlessness of summer sky. Yes, I had wings in this vision, and they unfolded, humongous and shimmering indigo, sweeping the islands and the sea. Below me, deep in the wave, the star responded frantically, desperately.

I did not need a boat or diving gear anymore. I folded my wings and plummeted, like a cormorant diving after her prey. The power took me down, into the heart of the wave, where the Slumbering Star rumbled and stirred. I had never healed anyone, but I would do my best.

But the deeper I dove, the smaller I felt. I was facing the star now, that vast being underwave, and I knew that the power of two people was not enough. Not nearly enough. Doubt rocked me.

My sense of my own vastness dwindled down to a mere sparkle. Winked out.

The star's magic roared in my mind, and suddenly I could not breathe. I was falling sideways into the long, long deep.

There was something solid under my back. My mouth tasted foul and my eyes felt congealed, but I pried them open. I was lying on the grass. I tried to turn my head to look at Semberí's hill, but all I could see was a shrouded, dark sky. I did not remember it being this late.

"She's coming to." Someone else spoke by my side. Veruma. She was crouching, and her worried face loomed over me. "Ranra, please. Say something."

I moved my lips gingerly. "Guano."

"Thank Bird." Veruma exhaled.

I managed to mutter, "Where's Lilún?"

"I'm here." Lilún's voice sounded broken. I couldn't see them, so I rolled over to my side, toward their voice. Pluck. I gulped for air, trying to fight down the pain.

Lilún crouched on the grass some distance away, knees pulled to their chest, their head to the side.

"How long was I out?" I asked.

"A few hours," said Lilún, not looking at me.

"We came here in the morning." More question than statement. "It's night." I had to get up, but my body screamed at me to stay put.

Veruma extended a hand to me, and groaning, I let her pull me up to a sitting position. "It's noon," she said.

"Then why is it dark like Bird's guano-crusted cloaca?"

Veruma frowned. "You should drink something first. I have water in my flask . . ."

"Plucking tell me," I croaked, but she thrust a silver flask into my hands. I drank ravenously, all the time watching Lilún. Something was off with them, I needed—

Veruma plucked the empty flask from my hand. "The Mother Mountain has spewed a cloud of ash."

What?

"I'm sorry for interrupting your tryst." She eyed us both. "Maybe next time you'll choose a . . . a different place for your experiments, so if something goes wrong, I can spot for you?"

"We didn't," I said. "We just kissed."

"And then you fell over, and were out for hours. I miss those days."

She jested, but her voice sounded sour, and I wasn't in the mood. I dragged myself up, walked a few steps toward Lilún, then collapsed at their side. They looked ashen.

"Were you out, too?" I asked them.

They rubbed their eyes. "I thought you'd died. You weren't breathing."

I'm fine. Nothing happened. Lines of bravado rose in my mind, but I didn't speak them. "We've almost done it. I almost succeeded, Lilún, and then I was falling. I thought I died, too."

"I'm sorry," they whispered. "I let you down. I could not hold it . . . not in the end, my magic unraveled, Ranra, and I . . ." They turned away. "I thought I killed you."

The realization struck me then, a terrible, corrosive feeling I'd never felt before. I'd endangered myself plenty, in play and in earnest, but it wasn't the same as endangering Lilún. I had risked their life without their explicit consent, without any negotiation, without preparation, on a whim. My stomach churned.

"No, it is I who let you down, Lilún—I was frivolous, reckless, I used your magic alone, when I already knew it would take a whole community . . ." I felt rattled by sudden fear. "It was too much for you—for any single person—to hold. You could have died. I am sorry . . ."

"It was my idea." Lilún touched my wrist lightly, a reminder. "I grabbed you. I drew on my magic."

I shook my head. "It was my decision."

"But, Ranra . . ."

"You asked me to lead, so now you cannot take responsibility for this failure. It is mine to shoulder."

There was nothing more to say. We sat together, my thigh touching theirs, their breathing and mine out of sync. I thought about Veruma, her uneasy laughter and her hints, and how she simply waited now, and my mood darkened further.

"I need to go," I told Lilún. "I need to understand what's happening with the Mother Mountain." And I needed to attend to Veruma, who'd sought me out and endured my brusqueness, but it wasn't fair to her. We weren't lovers at the moment, but she was family. I needed to talk to her about Lilún, and how she felt, not leave her to hang around for my convenience. "I can take you back to Keeper's House, Lilún. Or . . . home . . ."

Lilún laughed, unsteady. "You were dead a moment ago. Can you even walk?"

I'd rather walk than be dead. I pushed myself up, swayed, waved Veruma away. Steadied myself. My shoulders felt pounded by stones and my legs were heavy, but there was work to do.

We had almost succeeded. This is what I chose to think about. I could see, burned into my vision, the complex lines of light. There was a rhythm to this work, a resonance . . . I'd have to talk with Ulár about it, later.

"I'll be all right," I said. "But I want to help you."

Lilún smiled up at me, and I thought they would cry. "The hill is gone."

I looked around, again and again. Then back to them. "I am so sorry."

"No," they said. "I will rest here a bit and wait to see if they changed their mind. I can find my way back to Keeper's House."

"Are you sure?"

They nodded. "I'm sure. Just, just take care of yourself."

I bent over and kissed the top of Lilún's head. This

was exactly the wrong thing to do, because I almost toppled. My head spun.

Lilún squeezed my hand. "I'll be fine. Go, do."

Walking was bad, but it got better with practice. I was down the hill and headed southwest with Veruma before I realized that I didn't ask Lilún to come with me to the Mother Mountain. It felt like I had, but all I had offered them was home or Keeper's House. I wasn't even sure if they'd been home since the earthquake.

"Do you think I'm a bad person?" I asked Veruma.

"What are you talking about?" She sounded surprised.

"I should've talked to you more about Lilún, and to them about you."

Veruma shrugged. "You did. You asked me if I was jealous."

She made it sound like I'd made a selfish fool out of myself, which was the truth. I said, "You're right. I shouldn't have . . ."

Veruma laughed. "Is this an apology?"

"I left Lilún by the side of the plucking road."

"They said they wanted to be alone. They are an adult. You can't drag people around, Ranra." Veruma vented an exasperated sigh and walked faster. I struggled to keep up with her, my body still complaining with every step.

Much later, I realized that I had not actually apologized.

Lilún

When Ranra left with Veruma, I just slumped back to the grass, and breathed. It was good to lean against something that did not talk, did not expect me to go anywhere, did not want things from me. Did not run. Did not die.

The air was dark, and it smelled wrong. I wondered how far Ranra had gotten in her journey toward the Mother Mountain. Ranra had told me this was a regular hike, but I worried for her. She'd been dead, and I mourned her for hours, devastated and guilt-racked, and then she woke up and ran off. It was very much her style, but now my whole body shook, as if it had been flattened by an enormous weight and then abruptly released.

Something cold brushed my toes, and I opened my eyes to the canopy of quince trees, fruit hanging overhead. I had been transported back to the grove, to the exact spot I had been in before Semberí had banished us. My ancestor crouched by my side, the tatters of their semitransparent garment sweeping my feet. The ghost looked worried. "I can't believe she discarded you after all that."

With effort, I clambered up to a sitting position. I did not want to argue with Semberí, but they mattered to me, and so did Ranra, and I had to try, at least, to defend her. "This wasn't her idea. I asked to stay here, Semberí. Well, not here. At the foot of the hill, where I was after you threw us out."

"She just left you there. And still you defend her."

I could've gotten up and tried to leave, and a part of me wanted to, but it seemed like too much work. Perhaps if I tried, they'd just put me back outside.

I said, "You don't seem to think that I can or should have free will."

Semberí swayed left and right, rose up and floated between the quince boughs, then settled back at my feet before I so much as moved. They did not say anything.

I hugged my torso with my arms. "Is it because I've fallen in love with her, or because I follow her?"

They ignored my question. "If you follow her, then why did you stay?"

"When I get overwhelmed, I need to sit." *And also, I hoped you would open the hill again, but I did not expect you to toss me in and out like a doll.* I felt bitter now, and cold, and the smell in the air bothered me—a chalky, rotting odor that overpowered even the sea. It was hard to breathe here. I wanted to be somewhere else.

Semberí fell silent for a span of a few breaths. When they spoke, they appeared calmer. "I will tell you a story."

I wasn't sure if I had it in me to listen, but I could not move either. "Very well."

This close, Semberí's face appeared almost translucent. I could see the quince boughs through them, a few of the young fruit still clinging to branches.

"When I carried the star in my hands," they began, "I walked west, out of the great Burri desert, where a land dreamt itself into being between the very edge of the desert and the vast domain of the sea. It wasn't a large land, and it was both beauteous and discordant, mirroring the music of my own heart. Its bones sang to me with the colors of rainbow, and with the voice of spilled blood. There were groves of young fruit trees growing there, and encampments of people that came together to build a city yet unborn. I wanted to plant my star there. I wanted to stay among them, far enough from the vulnerable heart of the landmass, but the people would not let me.

"'You bring magic not of our making,' they said. All their leaders were men, and they would not allow ichidar to be known among them, let alone rule them. Women were praised, but I could see that the elders in their camps were afraid even of women's magic. They whispered between themselves, inventing unspeakable crimes that they wanted to become their law. They wanted—would you believe it, they wanted to burn out the deepnames of every woman who dared to take magic. They talked of such things in council, as if it was yet another matter to discuss, like the harvest.

"And yet, such beauty they made, Erígra, such jewels of emerald and ruby, such splendor of marble and sandstone. They hunted the great razu beast in the desert and brought its tusk to be carved into gates, and they fired clay bricks and chiseled stone for the harbor. If such a great artistry was theirs, perhaps they could be steered away from terrible deeds? They told me they needed no stranger to rule them. I said I did not wish to rule them, only to protect and plant my star, but they chased me away with threats of violence. Hundreds of years later, I learned the name of the city—Iyar, and its people, Iyari.

"On my way out of Iyar, I passed through a fruit grove. A child—I think an ichidi, because our people are everywhere, whether we are acknowledged by others or not—a small child put a piece of fruit into my pocket. Some fisherwomen took me in their boat across the narrow Stray Sea to the north, to the land of the marsh. I did not remember much of my earlier life, but I thought I had been born there. Yet, when I came back, the marsh was forlorn of people and full of strange sounds and ill vapors. I could not stay there. The fisherwomen had returned to Iyar, but my star sustained me and increased my magic. I walked over the wave to these isles.

"After I planted the star in the sea here, Erígra, its sustaining presence was removed from me, and I regained the use of my hands, which no longer cradled it. I had not eaten or slept for months, so I found a place to rest, on this very hill. Preserved by the star's magic, the fruit in my pocket had remained fresh."

Some memory stirred in me. Semberí's voice. *I carried a piece of rotten fruit when I walked on water . . .*

I raised my hand, almost unthinkingly. Semberí recoiled from me, floated up in the air. "Yes?" they hissed, clearly upset at being interrupted, but I could not stop myself.

"Was this the fruit in your song, the one I heard— you sang the fruit was rotten?"

Semberí hung frozen in the air above me, and only the hems of their garment made motions in the wind. At last, they said, "You are a poet. You figure it out."

"Sorry," I muttered. "Please continue . . ."

Semberí descended slowly to the ground, settled down, shaking their head. "Where was I? The fruit I carried over the wave. It was a quince. A fresh one. It was bumpy and strangely shaped, and many would call it ugly, but I was suddenly ravenous and shaking, and it beckoned to me. I bit into it. It was hard and sour, inedible. Seized by frustration, I threw the fruit on the ground and left the hill, thinking bitterly about Iyar and the child who had tricked me. But the islanders found me and welcomed me. They fed and sheltered me, and I did not think much more about the fruit.

"In a few years I came here again. Young saplings had grown from the discarded fruit, and despite myself, I began to tend them. The trees thrived, and later, my islander friends devised ways of cooking and fermenting the quince. The quince is the best of fruits, I came to believe, but it needed our effort.

"I kept coming here. I kept thinking. Did the child trick me or not? There was readily edible fruit in their grove, apples and apricots and plums for which the city of Iyar is now famous, but the child put a quince in my pocket while I could do nothing, because I held my star with both hands. I could not refuse or alter that gift. It must have held deeper meaning. For nine hundred and ninety-nine years I have lingered here, thinking about this mystery."

Semberí fell silent as I ruminated on the sadness and the music and the longing of their tale. I could not figure out its deeper meaning, either. The story was a gift as strange as the quince, and I should have left it at that. But I could not. "You asked the people of Iyar if you could plant the star, but you did not ask the islanders. You planted the star here before you even met them."

"It is so," said Semberí, not arguing, not denying, not explaining anything.

"You didn't ask for their consent."

"It is so," said Semberí again.

"And yet our people welcomed you."

"I could not have carried the star any farther." Semberí's form paled like dissipating smoke, then filled out again. "I had carried it for a long time by then, and knew it better, and knew myself better. It had to be planted, Erígra, and here, at the very edge of the naming grid of the land, was the safest place in case something went wrong."

I was trying to understand. "You thought it would die."

"As I carried the star, I grew to understand it. We . . . not conversed—communed."

"Then it was awake?" I wondered why it took them so long to tell me. "Was it consenting?"

"To be carried by me? Yes. But it wanted to die, by the end. It had hung too long by the Star of Despair, and the fellowship had tainted it. The star had despaired. It could not stop remembering terrible things, but it did not want me to see them. It grew worse after I left what is now the city of Iyar, after they rejected us, and then, when the marshy land I remembered as my home was inhospitable, the nightmares grew worse again. It was sheer pain to carry the star, especially over the sea."

"You endangered the isles and our unconsenting people." My voice sounded harsh and strange in my ears.

"You did not tell anybody this."

Finally, Semberí began to defend themself. "The magic of the star has enriched the islands. Its people grew prosperous. The fish in the sea multiply without end, and the land overflows with gardens. Trees thrive here, and their fruit are bountiful. Many named strong are born on these isles, and their powerful magic is nurtured by the star . . ."

I interrupted them. "The star could die at any moment, Semberí—but you weren't afraid for the people of these isles. They welcomed you, not knowing."

Semberí swirled in the air, agitated. "Not *at any moment*."

"No?"

"I was the first starkeeper, Erígra, I was one of the original twelve. You do not understand the power we had then, the deeds of creation—to shape the land, to form whole cities out of the amorphous desert—it is only here that I became mortal. A mortal of sorts."

Semberí wrung their vapor-soft hands. There was more to it. More.

I mouthed, "So what did you do?"

"The star needed a healer, but I could not heal it. It was not in me. But it trusted me, knowing that I carried it faithfully, in all its despair. It knew that I did not shy away from its pain, did not swerve from my devotion to it. It trusted me, so I did the thing I could do. I said to the Star of the Tides, *Go to sleep until a thousand years have passed since your hurt, since that worst day. Certainly a deep-minded healer will arise among these islanders and guide you to wholeness.*"

My head hurt and I wanted to scream, but I still had a question to ask. "And a year ago, you decided that it would be me?"

"You don't understand," the ghost said. "With each new starkeeper's ascension, I hoped and waited. I issued summons. Quite a few came to this hill, and I tried to tell them, to guide them. Some became starkeepers, others would not. It did not matter. They all did nothing."

I got up. "I am going to help Ranra, Semberí."

"The star needs a delicate touch. It needs you, not someone like her . . ."

"Nobody knows what it needs," I said. "Certainly even you don't."

I walked away from Semberí, down the hill, and they did not stop me.

Once I reached Keeper's House, Ulár rushed toward me, his long face animated with glee and sleepless agitation. "I figured it out!"

My mood, brittle after the conversation with Semberí was now unbalanced by Ulár's anxious buoyancy, and it took me a moment to reorient myself. "What?"

"The structure. I figured it out. It will take a crowd, all people with two and more deepnames—thank goodness there's a fair number of us . . . and we need to like each other . . ." Gesturing wildly, he led me to the council chamber, where other councilors were already assembled—Somay, Veruma, and a few others. Penár and Bodavar were still out on their mission to the outer islands. From the moment I saw him, Ulár never stopped talking. "First, those who have configurations with the longest and weakest deepnames need to connect with others who have longer deepnames . . . Here, I drew a chart!"

He grabbed a fresh-looking and somewhat messy chart from the table and pushed it into my hands, speaking faster and faster. "A person whose longest deepname is a three-syllable—for example, myself—connects to another person with a three-syllable . . ."

I struggled to follow Ulár's detailed explanation, but he kept speaking, oblivious to my difficulty. "Once I've formed the three-syllable connection, my three-syllable is *occupied*; now I can extend my two-syllable toward a different person whose longest deepname is a two-syllable; for example, you. I'm now connected to two people, not just one. And now that your longest deepname, which is your two-syllable, is *occupied*, you can connect your single-syllable to someone with a single-syllable; for example, Ranra . . ."

He pointed out the connections on the chart. I was starting to get the gist of it. A complicated, multifaceted net created by many people who all liked each other and worked together, beginning from the weakest, longest deepnames and progressing to the strongest and shortest. It sounded good, but somehow also dangerous, like a house made of carefully matched sticks that weren't glued or nailed together. Perhaps it would be enough if these pieces were safely joined, like artfully made pieces of wood that interlocked perfectly in the hands of a skilled and patient artisan . . .

"Have you tested this?" I asked, dubiously.

"Not entirely. I need you. Let's take Somay . . ."

Somay looked up from the chart, not quite happily. Their abstract ichar earring swung in their ear, the opal in it enticing me with its soft, multicolor shimmer. Somay grumbled, "Sure, Ulár, take me, why not."

"Apologies," said Ulár, but I wasn't sure that he paid much attention to Somay's tone. "With Somay's permission, let's take Somay, who like myself also has the Builder's Triangle of three-, two-, and one-syllable deepnames . . ."

Somay shrugged, but didn't protest. I could see that they had already practiced this, perhaps exhaustively, while I was at the grove. Both of them extended their Builder's Triangles, and after some friction and hesitation, their three-syllables latched together.

"Now," Ulár said, "my three-syllable deepname is *occupied*, and I am extending my two-syllable toward you!"

I had only ever connected with Ranra, and it was harder to connect to Ulár. He felt very linear, and buzzing with excitement, and not very welcoming, but I did like him. After a few attempts, our two-syllable deepnames connected.

Power streamed through me. I could now pull on it, take from both Ulár and Somay, use the magic to my own ends. I did nothing of the sort, but just through the connection, my vision became clarified and focused on magical power, while the mundane world dimmed. I saw the luminous deepname grids planted in the walls and foundations of Keeper's House by the strong builders of the past; and I saw, deep belowground, the faint shimmer of the naming grid of the land. Somewhere far and yet close, I felt the star. I tasted its fear and yearning under my tongue—astringent and deeply unbalancing, like a medicine that could just as easily kill you as heal you, and I felt that maybe I could—

Push and pull. Push and pull. I felt it in my bones. A gentle, attuning motion was needed.

I would match myself to the star, match my breathing, my being, and guide it until it breathed calmness like I breathed, until it was pacified. I breathed in and out, trying to hold on to calm. Suddenly my eyes, my ears, my mouth, my nose, my fingers all filled with a sense of wailing, as if an enormous boom were approaching from the sky, a wave of sound that warped the air, tore glass from the soaring buildings of steel, uprooted trees— and then it hit and hit and hit and hit, staggering me, piercing my body with shards.

I had to remain calm. I had to take a step forward. To absorb this into myself, to carry all this pain and despair in my arms. I needed to carry it, like Semberí had carried it, for as long as it took.

I hesitated. In front of me, the sea churned like a vortex opening into the abyss. Waves of fear battered me. I had to guide the star, to breathe calmness to it, but I wasn't that strong. I wasn't strong at all. My existence was meaningless—meaningless—

I yanked myself back, disengaging from the star and from the structure, gasping for breath. My lips formed the words, "I cannot—"

Ulár patted me on the back. "We did great. Now we make charts, handpick the people, practice—"

"I don't know if this can be done," I whispered.

Ulár grinned at me. "We're doing it."

"No, I mean . . . I think I tried to do it and couldn't. For the person who leads . . . there is just too much . . ." Semberí had carried the star, but that was a thousand years ago. *There is too much despair now*, I thought. *And Semberí never attempted to heal it* . . .

Ulár shrugged my words off. "Ranra will do it. She is the one. But first, we would need to create as many connections as possible, with as many people as possible, and then we all generate the power and give it to Ranra . . ."

I did not argue with him, but my stomach churned.

Sometime later, Ranra and Veruma returned from the Mother Mountain. Ranra looked ashen-faced, but determined. Veruma just looked ashen.

"The mountain's fire is awake," Ranra reported, without a greeting. "The mountain feels different—well, I'm sure you all know me, you know she always felt parental to me. She feels agitated now, buzzing. Fire and ash are coming through fissures. I don't know what can turn this back—but the fire is a danger to the city. We definitely don't have a year."

"Perhaps if we switched our studies to the mountain, we could figure out how to pacify it, buy ourselves more time," said Somay.

Ranra's voice brooked no argument. "The issue is not pacifying the mountain—the mountain is connected to the star, tethered to it, just like I'm tethered to it. Who placed the tether there, I don't know—but healing the star will help the mountain."

"If you say so," said Somay. "I've been a voice of doubt in your councils, Keeper, and I will continue to be. We must place alarm stations at the mountains: named strong who would sound the shofar longhorn, deep-name-amplified, to warn the city if it gets much worse."

"Do it," Ranra said. "Your voice of doubt is the voice of our need, and I am grateful for it."

Before Somay had a chance to respond, Ulár spoke up, his excitement undampened by Ranra's report. "No, we figured out how to make the big plan work. Look . . ."

He showed Ranra the new chart, and for a while there was nothing to be heard except Ulár's rapid speech, interrupted by Ranra's questions, and the sound of charts being moved.

In the end, she took a deep breath. "The work you have done is incredible. But this—this requires all of us to perfectly coordinate. If one person topples, everything topples?"

"Not . . . necessarily," said Ulár, scratching his head. "I need to build some give into the method. We need to do some experiments to see what happens if someone, say, faints . . ."

"And how exactly would you do these experiments?" said Somay. "Hit them about the head?"

Ranra stared at them for a moment, then turned back at Ulár. "The issue is this, Ulár. When I formed this structure last with Erígra, the mountain's fire was awakened. It might have been a coincidence, but—this work feels big to me. Dangerous. I need you to look for alternatives to this method. We also need more time to understand the discovery."

"I agree that the structure is dangerous," I chimed in. "When we experimented here, I saw—"

Ulár spoke over me. "We'll figure everything out before we come together for you."

"Ulár," Ranra said, her voice steely. "You must look for another way, a less dangerous way, and you must also get the structure ready. Both things must happen now, and they must happen quickly. I'm sorry I have to press you when you are not getting sleep, but . . ."

Ulár just grinned. "This is the most beautiful thing in magical geometry since the Birdcoming. There's nothing better than this. I promise."

Ranra looked suddenly exhausted. There was a vertical crease on her forehead I had not noticed before. She said, "You promise."

"I promise," Ulár repeated.

Ranra and I exchanged glances. Ulár was a genius, but both of us had touched the star, and both of us now felt the fear.

Variation the Fourth:
RUGÁR

I am both bears

Ranra

The trip up the mountain had terrified me. The welcoming, soothing feeling of her was gone, and she felt—not angry, but desperate, like a person who had seen their worst fears emerge from the ground, inescapable. The ash and gas themselves were not as bad as she felt, and I couldn't stop thinking I'd caused this.

When I tried to explain, Veruma made callous comparisons to my mother until I told her to shut it. With her two weaker deepnames, Veruma could not feel this the same way I did—the fear, the endless churning fear from the mountain. Perhaps I was putting too much of my own emotion into how I saw the mountain, but she mattered to me, and now she hurt. What fool had tethered her to the star? Was it that ghostly piece of floating guano, Semberí? And why would they do that?

My advisors looked about as agitated as the Mother Mountain. Veruma, who'd seemed so determined on our way up the mountain, was now shaken and silent. Somay's face was scrunched as if they had bitten into a raw etrog. Lilún looked scared and small, huddled in their chair. Ulár alone seemed in good spirits, perhaps overly so. His cheeks burned, as if he was drunk on his discoveries. His eyes glistened with a feverish light. These episodes were familiar to me from our long friendship, and did not worry me much before now, but this wasn't a good thing. I could order him to rest, force him even, and he would find ways to work where I could not see him. Or I could leave him to his work.

I felt the star now in my bones, felt its reverberation in my teeth—the deep, angry rumbles that had disturbed the Mother and made her spout ash and foul gasses. I needed Ulár to do his work, but this work could further unbalance the star, and the mountain with it.

I did not want to come to this so fast. I had barely started my keeperdom. Semberí—that Bird-pecked fool of a ghost—had insisted we'd had a year. Perhaps if I'd done nothing at the foot of their hill, we'd have that year. But I doubted it.

I attempted to steady myself. "Ulár, I appreciate your work, and its urgency. You can chart and plan, but please do not experiment without me."

"You want me to discover two separate methods without experimenting. How do you expect me to do that?" Ulár sounded reasonable enough, but I doubted he could feel the star's distress as acutely as I did now.

"I am concerned about us unbalancing the star ever more. The whole thing is fragile."

"I understand, Keeper, but the method must involve experiments if I . . ."

"Veruma." She didn't look good. I needed to check

in with her, I needed to let her rest, but there was no time and no rest now for any of us. "Veruma, please keep an eye on Ulár. If he begins to experiment without me, hit him about the head."

"But, Ranra . . ." Ulár and Veruma protested in unison. A crooked grin split Somay's face, but they said nothing.

"I am the starkeeper," I said. "This is an emergency. I hate to do this, but I must. Chart, plan, do not experiment." I needed to eat something, change my clothing, but there was no time. "Erígra, with me."

My lover clambered out of their chair and followed me out of the council chamber. We were alone in the corridor when Lilún tapped me on the shoulder. "I'm happy to see you, and I'm happy to support you. But please don't give me orders? At least, not so brusquely? You could simply ask me."

"I'm sorry," I began. Was I sorry? I wasn't sure. None of them felt the agitation the way I did, I, who was tethered to the Sputtering Star, and connected to Mother Mountain since childhood. "You've been told that we have a year, and for all I know you believe it, but we don't. This is an emergency, Lilún." An emergency in which we needed to act in unison or we would not make it. The islands had weathered storms and earthquakes before, but I was terrified. We had always come together and rebuilt. We trusted our magics and our friendships, our warmth and our gardens, our abundance, our scholarship, but that wouldn't be enough now. And Ulár's plan required perfect coordination, a singular focus. It was easier to imagine a shoal of fish moving in unison than a group of islanders. I could not even keep my advisors together in the same room.

I said, "Speaking of which, have you seen Dorod lately? I must speak to them right away."

"I haven't seen Dorod," said Lilún. "But I think they are at the harbor . . ."

"Let's go, then," I said impatiently.

"Ranra," said Lilún. "We need to talk, but you need to slow down."

Why couldn't they understand? This wasn't a calm, quiet night we had to ourselves, we didn't have the luxury of a gentler pace. "There is no time to slow down, Lilún, I must see Dorod."

"Why do you even want me to come with you?"

"Because I love you." The words fell from my mouth unbidden, but I had no wish to take them back. "And I trust you more even than I trust Veruma, and I trust her with my life."

Lilún waved a hand, exasperated. "You say you love me, but we've only been together a few days, how can you know anything in a few days? I want to be with you, but you just keep running . . . I cannot go this fast. You were dying just a few hours ago, and still you keep pushing, pushing . . ." Their voice wavered, as if they would break into tears, or scream. "I need you to listen—when the magics came together—when Ulár and I experimented with Somay—just with the power of two people, I tried—I saw—I was scalded by the star's pain . . . When we all come together for you, when we give you our magics, it will be amplified thousandfold. Have you considered how you'd go about this healing?"

"You said you'd support me," I said gruffly.

"I do." Tears were running down their face now. "I will freely give you my power. But this doesn't need force, Ranra, it needs quietude, it needs attunement, it needs time, Ranra . . ."

"I wish we had the time." I grabbed them by the shoulders. "Love, I wish you and I could have all the time in the world, I want to take you sailing, I want to sit quietly with you and study healing books and talk about the very best method to accomplish this task, but it's going to Bird-plucking blow up if we cannot stop it, Lilún, and I need to plucking know what all my three-named strong are doing, and that includes Dorod!" I was shouting. I didn't want to shout at Lilún.

They pushed away, out of my grip, and simultaneously I let them go. "I'm sorry," I said. "You're right. I am sorry. I'll talk to you later." I turned and ran toward the exit, not even looking back.

Outside of Keeper's House, the air was clearing, but I could still see the gray clouds over the Mother Mountain, and smell the burnt, foul odor. My agitation kept building as I walked toward the harbor, nodding curtly to people I met. I saw no more smiles, no more offers of quince wine or dough pockets—everybody, the named strong and magicless people alike, looked disturbed and worried. Many of the rebuilding sites I had visited just yesterday were abandoned today, as if the whole of Gelle-Geu was holding its breath for a better hope to appear.

But when I reached the harbor, I found plenty of people there, rushing around with serious and determined faces. Many were loading up the boats and ships, or tinkering with repairs. Gulls circled ravenously over the crowd, looking for scraps. The tradeships that Penár and Bodavar had taken to the outer islands were back now, and islanders from Agara and Mehmey were helping to load supplies. At the center of this activity was Dorod, surrounded by their crew and talking animatedly with about a dozen people when I approached.

Dorod looked as good as usual, solid and distinguished-looking in a splendid brown korob with silver embroidery around the shoulders. Their posture was as proud as ever, their expression as self-assured. Their gray hair was braided in the five-way fashion, with a dozen or more rugár tokens woven in, so that their hair resembled a silvery thicket full of bears. I wish I could be reassured by that sight, and maybe I was, but first I wanted to know the meaning of all this activity.

"Ranra." Dorod bowed to me without any shade of either subservience or condescension. "My greetings."

I didn't feel like small talk, and my nod in their direction was curt. I replied, "You haven't shown up in my councils."

"No, Ranra. We do not have the time."

"You think all is lost." I could see that.

"No," they said. "I don't."

"You think I'm a child, Dorod, and do not understand what you are trying to accomplish here? Your seven tradeships as large as ever graced these islands, and completely unnecessary for our trade—you built them rapidly over the last few years—but however large and splendid they might be, your ships won't carry even half of our people to safety, not even a third—"

"Not even that," said Dorod. "Not nearly that many." They looked me straight in the eye without humor, without sadness, without anger. "You will be surprised, but most people are at home. Many don't believe that anything is amiss except for regular fluctuations of weather. And we have had earthquakes before, and so many islanders are simply preparing to endure. But those with powerful magic can really feel it now, and there will be many who'll eagerly go to the ships. Some will survive if we're lucky. Begin again."

"Is that it? Is that your whole plan?" I wanted to shout, and managed just barely to hold back. "You should've come to my councils, helped us build the structure. The disaster can be averted—it is not too late, and I need every named strong—and especially the three-named strong, there aren't even sixty of us on the archipelago, all told, and every single three-named strong maximizes our chances, increases the connections we can make . . ." Dorod listened, as stolidly as before, until I ran out of steam.

"Four years ago," said Dorod, "when Terein was still hiding out in his rooms, refusing to acknowledge how close we were to disaster, I went to see him. 'Find a deep-minded and patient person inclined to the healing arts, and some powerful named strong who can support them, then gently but quickly train them, and learn all the ways in which the star can be helped,' I said to the old Keeper, but he said, 'The less we poke the swarm of bees, the less likely we are to be bitten.'"

I said, "No. He knew. But he despaired entirely and

thought all was lost. He wrote me a letter."

"That was later," Dorod said. "Listen. Please."

I nodded.

Dorod continued their tale. "I came back a few weeks later. 'The Mother Mountain overgrows with pines,' I said, 'and I would like to cut some of them down to build new tradeships.' Eventually, we came to an agreement." Dorod waved their hand at the newly finished seventh ship that towered proud at its pier, its multiple masts a complex latticework of connections. "I obtained some detailed Iyari tradeship designs, and remade them until I was happy. In another year, we would have two more ships, if we're lucky, but both the pines and the patience of my workers would run out at that point."

"I do not think we have a year." I kept saying this, but I had no idea why. Was I afraid that nobody believed me? Or that I was to blame for time running out? "I do wonder if our experiments hastened this." In truth, I had no way to know whether or not our meddling had made any difference in the time we had left. "Would you rather we did nothing, like Terein? Buy more time for your ships? Would you rather I was a different person, a . . . a deep-minded healer or some such?"

"I am a big believer in this—" said Dorod. "Those who show up to the work are entitled to it. I would much rather have a leader who tries to prevent a disaster and puts all their heart into it, than one who despairs and hides out in their room. Though I respect it as a personal choice."

"Where . . . where would we even go?" My voice squeaked. Dorod had mentored and supported me after I left my mother's house, and sometimes I still felt young and inexperienced next to them, even though I was a woman at the height of my power.

Dorod said, "We would sail east. If we survive. Over the wave, back to the landmass. I hear there's a long stretch of marshy coast to the northeast from here. Ill vapors are rumored to poison the soil and the air. Nobody lives there, so we won't need to fight anyone, and there's all kinds of ways to get rid of vapors."

I felt like I was going to throw up. "Do you think we stand no chance?" I asked again.

"On the contrary," said Dorod. "Your plan is just daring and utterly reckless enough to work, and I hope, by Bird's whirlwind plumage, that you succeed. But we'll have a huge problem then." They paused, for full effect. "Too many tradeships, not enough trade to support them." Dorod grinned, and that eased my mind a little.

"Is there something I can help you with? More supplies? More workers?"

"I have what I need," said Dorod. "But if I were you, I would establish a chain of command. It's not an islander thing, but we have to know what to do if there won't be enough time for community decisions. So assign an eram—a wartime leader—to each ship. We haven't had erams for hundreds of years, but we might need them now. We have seven large ships. I'll take the new one, you'll take another—so assign five more people."

I said, "Not all of my councilors know how to steer a ship—Veruma does, but I'm not sure about the others. Penár, Bodavár—they can hold their own. That leaves

Somay and Ulár, who don't know their boat from their goat."

Dorod shrugged. "My crew will help with the mechanics. But each eram must be a three-named strong who can power the navigation. And first, they should be able to steer the people to their ship. The ones you named are known to me as powerful and decisive named strong, but they must be prepared to bring people on board quickly and in an orderly fashion. Bird willing, none of this will be necessary."

"I understand." In the pit of my stomach, fear churned and warred with the desire to act, to steer us toward my own vision. My way was much better than this.

Dorod grasped me by the arm. "Go do your thing. I will be here if you fail."

I bid Dorod farewell and walked away. In moments, they called my name again. "Ranra?"

"Yes?"

Their face twisted in some indescribable emotion. "Do not fail."

Lilún

I stepped out of the gloom of Keeper's House into the courtyard, then stopped, shielding my eyes from the bright sun that broke through the ashen cloud. Ranra was already gone. She'd said she loved me, and I felt so indignant at first. Perhaps she was one of those people who fell in and out of love easily.

I wanted to be with her, but it scared me. Perhaps I was the one who wanted something fleeting, something which was safe because it was fleeting. I wanted to go back to my house and lock the door for a month until things went back to what they were before. But everything was different now. I promised Ranra that I'd follow her to the harbor, but I could break my promise at any time. That was my freedom, my consent to give and withhold as I wanted.

I did not want either to give or to withhold. I wanted—I needed slowness, and my house, and my notebook to write the things that I witnessed when I joined forces with Ulár and Somay. I needed not to be around people so much. I wanted to be alone with my thoughts. These were my newly recognized, always present zúr turtle ways. I needed things to be safe.

It's going to plucking blow, she'd said. And I had promised to support her.

I sighed, exasperated with myself, and headed to the harbor.

The cloud of ash from the Mother Mountain had tattered into cloudlets. Halfway to the harbor I saw a broad-shouldered person walking briskly toward Keeper's House, and my breath caught. It was one of my dads, Veseli, coming this way. He spotted me, too, and we ran toward each other. He looked older now, his cloud of curls completely gray and floating above his head, undefeated; his face sported many more wrinkles. We embraced, then he pushed me away to take a look at me.

"Lilún, thank Bird! I went to your house. My heart

was about to leap out of my chest when I saw the wreckage—the neighbors told me you were at Keeper's House."

"I'm fine." I wasn't, but it didn't matter. "How did you get here?"

"Councilor Penár came in one of those giant ships, with supplies. I begged her to let me come back and find you." To my unspoken question, he said, "Meron and Genet are fine, they send their love . . . they thought you'd be all right, but I worried."

I pulled him to me. He was taller, and broader, his clothes smelled of sea salt, and his arms held me tight. Just what I needed.

When we separated, I felt better. "I lost the token," I said inconsequentially. "The token you left me—it's zúr."

He kissed me on the top of my head. "I'm glad you figured it out."

"Dad Veseli . . ." I wanted to tell him so much, but now that I felt better, I remembered that I promised Ranra I'd follow. "Dad, I need—I'm involved in, I . . ." I mumbled. "I'm with the Keeper, I promised her I would help . . ."

"Go, do," he said, much as I had to Ranra, earlier.

"Go on to Keeper's House, tell them I asked them to find room for you. I'll see you later." A quick embrace, and once again I walked, with much more spring in my step, to the harbor.

The clouds still crowded the sky, but the sun shone defiantly upon the grand trading ships and the smaller boats anchored there. I circled around, but saw no sight of Ranra. Instead, I found Dorod—at a center of a small crowd, directing workers. In Dorod's hair, a gathering of brass bears jangled companionably.

I waved at them. "Have you seen Ranra? She was looking for you . . ."

"I just talked to her," said Dorod. "She ran off, our Ranra." Dorod motioned somewhere west, toward the center of Gelle-Geu.

I looked at the workers and the goods they were moving —loads of dried figs and salted fish, great clay bottles of water. "Are you sending more help to Agara Island?" I asked them.

"I'm making sure we have more than one future."

My mood soured once more. "You don't believe that Ranra's plan will be successful."

Dorod laughed briefly, then their face sobered. "Funny, she said the same thing. I have no idea what is going to happen with your plan. I'm glad she has a plan. Just a few months ago, the only plan in these isles was mine, and I'm not about to abandon it just because you youngsters took a few days to hatch another."

I did not quite know what to say. "The old Keeper didn't think—"

"Terein thought we should all just die, quickly and without too much worry. I had to convince him to let me build these ships. So it doesn't matter what Terein thought."

"And Ranra?"

"Look. It would have been best to put a few years of planning into the magical working you all have devised. But I am not trying to convince Ranra to abandon it. When Terein chose inaction, Ranra at least argued with him. Everybody else just watched, content to sip their wines and wait for someone more decisive to come along and do the work. And that's our Ranra."

Hearing her name on Dorod's lips eased my mind. I wanted to sit down with Dorod, have a real conversation. I wanted to ask Dorod if they thought that Ranra would leave me, but now wasn't the time, not with everything changing. Dorod's bear tokens shone in the setting sun. Two days ago, I'd returned briefly to my house for supplies. I found the clothes covered in debris in my courtyard, but my brass token wasn't there.

I said, "I lost my zúr turtle after the earthquake. My fathers gave it to me, but I only wore it for one day, because I'd just figured out my variation . . . because of you, actually . . ."

Dorod smiled in encouragement, and I babbled on. "One of my dads is here now, but I couldn't even show him . . . I keep thinking, if I knew how to braid it properly in my hair, I wouldn't have lost it—and now it is gone, and so many other things . . ."

"Easily remedied." Dorod called out to someone, and in a few moments an ichidi I didn't know came back with a large bird's-eye maple box full of tokens, all brass, and a large horn comb. Dorod selected a turtle token, more abstract and angular than the one I'd lost.

"Here," they said. "Sit on this."

I sat on a large wooden crate among other boxes being loaded, and Dorod strung the turtle onto a thin blue cord, then tied two knots on each side of it. "May I comb out your hair?"

I gulped down tears. Nodded.

Dorod began to brush, tugging at my hair gently, but firmly. The sun streaked down upon us, and around us, a small crowd of ichidar gathered to witness. Tears streamed down my face openly now. I told myself earlier that I wanted to be alone, but this felt important. This was my true ceremony, declaring myself in truth and being guided and witnessed by my people. It made me feel dizzy and warm, and not able to say much.

Dorod had no trouble speaking. "The shorter hairstyle you have can be challenging for tokens, and that's why you need the help of the cord. You first secure the cord itself at the base of your skull, and then braid around it. If you find a token without a hole, you can knot the cord around it, like this." They selected a different turtle from the box, and showed me how to form a proper holding knot.

I thought about Ranra's words, and said, "Thank you for doing this, but . . . but isn't this the wrong time?" It felt self-indulgent and strange not to rush, to sit here among this warmth and care when I should be running somewhere.

Dorod resumed their work, brushing out my hair. Their motions had rhythm, and their arms were so steady and big, and their presence behind me was solid. I thought once again about their ichidi variation. Rugár—*I am both bears*—at once both father and mother, protective and caring and steady in their fierceness.

They said, "Let me tell you a story."

I breathed, and my eyes closed, attentive only on the rhythm of Dorod's brushing, and their words.

"Many of us have two names because our parents gift us with an outer and an inner name, a name for the world and a name to share with one's loved ones. Some, like Ranra, are given a nickname they do not much like. A few of us, like myself, mark their lineage."

Dorod's hand brushed my forehead, gathering a strand of hair. I wanted to stay like this forever, centered and cared for, with my eyes closed. Among people, but not overwhelmed.

"I am Dorod Laagar because my great-grandmother was called Laaguti Birdwing. She died when I was eight, but I remember many of her stories. She was a great rebel who fled the city of Iyar with a crew of other magically powerful women. In Iyar, see, women are not allowed to hold deepnames. So the ruler of Iyar imprisoned them, but Laaguti and her friends fought their way out. Not everyone made it, but these women did. If you let me guide your hands, I will teach you how to braid your token."

"Yes," I mumbled.

Dorod's hands were calloused and warm, and they guided me through the motions of twisting and rebraiding my hair with the cord and the turtle token properly positioned. I felt floaty, as if I was dreaming, and in my reverie I saw them as a bear, coming down the mountain in summer, with berries jangling like ichidi tokens in their fur.

"The Iyari rebels came here in a small ship, much smaller than my tradeships. As a child, I was fascinated by this history. Grandmother Laaguti told me that back in Iyar they do not recognize ichidar. That she had to learn about ichidar when she came here. She told me that in Iyar they used force to strip powerful women of their deepnames, and told them that to be disempowered was Bird's own gift to womankind. That's why my great-grandmother was a rebel. She was a three-named strong, like me." Dorod tugged on my hair, correcting one last imperfection. "It's done."

I got up dizzily, touching the turtle now nestled securely between locks of my bleached and braided hair. The charmed time was over, and I should have begun to rush, but my legs and my lips were woolen. "Thank you. Thank you so much, but I still don't know why you'd do this, especially now . . ."

"Our gardens, our learning, our magics—all that is good and fine," said Dorod with a firmness. "But above it all, we must remember who we are. We are fierce and free in our loves and our choices, and nobody rules us, not even the Keeper. We come together in councils and we choose our leaders, but none of them would even imagine taking our deepnames away, or indeed our ichidi tokens. We gift all to each other. Unless we perish, every single one of us, nobody and nothing can destroy this."

I found Ranra in one of the central streets of Gelle-Geu, at an outdoor market now empty of sellers and wares. More precisely, I did not find Ranra, I saw her. She had clambered on top of a bunch of stones that had fallen out of a nearby building, too big to easily restore or remove. Over her head, her Royal House was engaged, a bright warm triangle of magic that illuminated her figure and amplified the sound of her words. Around her, a crowd of townspeople gathered, listening, murmuring.

I was far enough to catch only snippets—" . . . a new magical construct that will give us a chance to pool our magics . . . we must act together as a community of people who care deeply about these isles, who are willing to put hope and love into the hardest work . . . there are risks—I do not want you to think otherwise, especially because we cannot test this without increasing our risk . . . I need anybody who is willing to add their power in this construct, but especially any two-named and three-named strong . . . After this is done, we will rebuild even brighter, I promise you that—and we will have the biggest gathering these islands have ever known, I will empty the Keeper's coffers, quince wine will run like a river, dumplings will grow on trees, we will be reveling for months!"

People cheered, I wasn't sure if at her vision of the party, or at a relief of having a plan of action laid out before them. Probably both. I hated gatherings, but right now I would give much to be at this gathering, victorious, my city shining as before, a glass of quince wine in my hand, if only to put the wine down and walk back to my house relieved and buzzing and full to bursting with lines of poetry. Or I could be with Ranra, and we could begin again where we'd been when the earthquake hit. In my pool, or on the starlit boat ride Ranra promised, or on that secret beach I found where every grain of sand was shaped like a very small star . . . and perhaps even Semberí would relax and wish us well and . . .

"Lilún." It was Ranra. She had spotted me in the crowd and came over, a grin on her face. "They are volunteering. We'll have plenty of people. Hundreds. We are lucky in our power, our community."

I spoke, swallowing tears. "We gift all to each other."

"I love your poetry so much," she said.

"That wasn't me. It was Dorod." I touched my new brass token. It had angles, not sharp, but interesting.

It was getting darker now, the longest day yielding into the embrace of the night. From afar, the mountain rumbled, and we both stared uneasily in its direction. Then Ranra laughed. "Are you still angry at me? I love what you did with your hair."

"That was also Dorod." But I took her hand in mine. "I'm not angry anymore. I'm glad you are doing this."

She beamed at me. "Let's go back to Keeper's House, get something to eat."

"My dad is there—Veseli—I would like you to meet him . . ."

She opened her arms and we came together, clasping each other, heart to a beating heart. Quite a few people cheered. I didn't care anymore. I felt surrounded by Ranra, by my people, poised between the anxiety of waiting and the certainty of action. For the moment, I was warm and cherished and safe.

We had dinner in the library room at Keeper's House, where the seats were deep and comfortable. Dad Veseli and Ranra took to each other, and regaled each other with jokes as we dined on braised fish and bright greens. After dinner, dad Veseli left for his guestroom. With his single three-syllable deepname, he would be no help with our structure. Ranra and I worked into the night. I told her about my vision of the star, and we looked at healing books together to try to puzzle it out. We found no great secrets there. If anybody had applied the healing arts upon the twelve primeval stars before, we did not find out.

I woke up in the darkened library room when Ulár brought finalized charts of all the people who volunteered to join our structure. Ranra seemed wide awake. She crouched by a low table, where Ulár spread his charts and began to explain them. "There will be seven of us in the core group—you, myself, Somay, Veruma, Erígra, Penár, Bodavar. Then the others—we have two hundred and forty in total . . . potentially . . ."

"You could connect more people if you opened the structure a bit more beyond our core group." Ranra tapped his chart with her pen. I was trying to sit up.

Ulár said, "Remember, these connecting must all like each other, which complicates the construct significantly. I personally have trouble connecting to people I don't know very well, even if I like them—so does Erígra . . ."

For a moment, I gave up on my attempts to sit, and nestled deeper into the cushions. Why were there cushions here? I wasn't sure, and didn't care. I would sit up any moment now, take a look at Ulár's charts . . . There was a blanket over me now, cozy, soft . . .

"Shhh, Erígra is asleep . . ."

I wasn't asleep.

"We can include more people, but the connections will be less tight, less practiced—it's a risk, Ranra . . . more raw power, but it will be unstable . . ."

Their voices faded in and out.

"You are at the pinnacle of this structure . . . you must be connected to those you like and trust the most."

"Veruma, Erígra, and you." Ranra's voice.

"Two of those are two-named strong, which would limit the available connections—consider a three-named strong, Somay, perhaps . . ."

"But you just said . . ."

I sank deeper into the cushions.

Ranra

The preparations took days, and we needed each one. Dorod wanted to send two tradeships to the outer islands, but I needed Penár here for the structure. We argued bitterly until Lilún's father, Veseli, volunteered to go back and work with our plan. He said, "There are many named strong on the outer isles. We will organize—and if need be, we will mount the ships. Do your work here."

After he left, Lilún was in tears, but not, I thought, out of hopelessness. Their face was full of light. And I wanted—without reason—to share some of that, so I made my way to my mother's house, alone and unaccompanied by Veruma this time, to try to convince her to prepare to leave if need be.

Adira was still in the same place, sitting at the same potter's wheel under the burning and overcast sky. A large group of women was with her now. Some were spinning, others carved spoons and little bows from wood, yet others sat idle, chewing on the candied rind of citrus.

"You always had an active imagination," my mother said. "This is just weather."

"The mountain . . ." I began.

"You always had a sense of overblown importance, Ranra," my mother said. "Taking too many deepnames certainly didn't help, let alone becoming a *Keeper*."

One of the women spoke up, in a soothing tone of voice. "I read in a book how three hundred years ago there was a similar eruption. Two months later everything was fine again."

Another said, "My mother told me that her grandmother remembered smoke coming from the mountain. It settled after a while."

They all nodded.

Four days later, I was awoken by a tremendous explosion that shook me out of the bed and onto the floor. Lilún woke up screaming, and I threw up my Royal House to shield them from flying debris. Keeper's House was the most solid and magically potent building in Gelle-Geu, but I could feel the foundations of it rumble. I took the disoriented Lilún by the hand, and together we made it out of the room, through the corridors full of frightened, screaming people, out into the courtyard.

Clouds of ash churned in the sky, obscuring the sun. In the distance, a red conflagration sprouted at the peak of the Mother Mountain. We were, most decisively, out of time.

I noticed Somay and Penár in the crowded courtyard, and made my way to them. Somay was dressed in red, to be easily spotted, they explained. We had agreed that the courtyard of Keeper's House would be the place for our work. It was wide, well-sheltered, made to host a large gathering, and whatever could topple there had toppled already.

"Where are the other erams? Where is Ulár?" I asked. They didn't know.

I said, "Here is Erígra, please keep together and do not separate. I must find Ulár, Veruma, and Bodavar." I planted a quick kiss on Lilún's cheek and ran off. Bird willing, we would have more time, and I would make it all up to them somehow. A hundred starlit walks. Two hundred poetry nights, five thousand dinners for just the two of us. Perhaps we could even pull on our configurations together to construct a bondage of light.

In the street people shied away from me, and I rubbed my mouth to wipe off the odd grin.

I found Bodavar first, running around with some children in tow. In the last few days, I had asked all of them to speak to the people, like Dorod had advised, and it was a relief to see that preparations had been put in place. I waved all our named strong toward the Keeper's House courtyard, where Somay's bright red korob shone like a beacon in the pressing crowd.

Ulár had been looking for me, it turned out, charts in hand. He, too, was found and herded in the right direction. That left Veruma. Where was Veruma? I had not seen her since I sent her to talk to her people, and I had not talked to her at any length since our trek up the Mother Mountain. Veruma could take care of herself, but my stomach churned with worry.

I found her at last in a little side yard by a broken fountain from which water gurgled freely onto the stones. She didn't even turn when I approached, and my heart sank. "Soli, love . . ." That name, which she'd asked me not to use with her, just spilled from my lips.

She turned. Her face was stricken and angry. "Don't talk to me like that. I had asked you, time and time again, not to call me Soli. And don't pretend that you love me."

"You are my best friend, Veruma. I love you. And often you are my lover." I chewed my lips. "The mountain is erupting."

"Pluck the mountain," Veruma said. "Pluck it all."

I took a deep breath and resisted screaming, *This is not the time*. We were on Veruma's time now, but I tried to push anger away. "You *are* jealous." She had assured me she wasn't, but what else could it be? She knew very well that I was multiple in my loves. She was too. Most islanders were. Except that most of my dalliances were brief, an evening's pleasure or a week's. Veruma was different. So was Lilún, and it would make sense that Veruma would feel weird about it. Yes, we needed to talk it out, but by Bird, not *now* . . .

"No, I'm not jealous, Ranra. I like and respect Erígra, and I'm not even with you anymore. I don't see why I should be jealous even if I was with you. No, it's the guano way you've treated me. Take me here, go with me there, do this, do that, talk to these people, don't talk to those people, and by the way, here's your place in the plucking chart, even though you're weaker than anybody else!"

"I have never said that!" I protested.

"No, but you think it, every single time. Yes, I have a Princely Angle, not a three-name configuration . . ."

"Erígra has the same configuration," I blurted, regretting it at once.

"Erígra could take the Royal House any day," said Veruma, "and when you talk to them, you do more than order them around, you stop and listen. Sometimes." She snorted. "It would have been nice if you stopped for a moment to talk to me, and not just when you needed me to run your errands!"

"I'm sorry," I said. She was right, but Bird peck it, my people had an amazing sense of timing. Why wouldn't they get that *things were going to blow?*

"I'm not jealous, Ranra, I'm angry."

"I get it," I said. "Tonight, working with Ulár, I decided that I would connect to the three people closest to me. I chose you, Ulár, and Erígra. Do you wish to reconsider?"

"What?" Veruma said.

I bit back *Ulár thought Somay would be a better choice.*
Tried for a calmer tone. "Veruma, I love you, and I understand that you think I screwed up, which I would be more than happy to acknowledge and work on after this is done, because the Bird-forsaken mountain is erupting NOW!" A second explosion punctuated my words, but I felt it before it happened, felt it through my connection to the star. The star was tethered to the mountain.

"Oh, all right, have it your way," Veruma said.

We made it back to the courtyard, but doubt churned in me. Strong gusts of wind were hitting the courtyard now, stirring clouds of thin dust. Ulár was arranging people in patterns which would put them as close as possible to their deepname partners, a complicated process in which he was utterly absorbed. I pulled him aside, nonetheless. "How are we doing?" I asked.

"We had two hundred and forty on the list, but right now we only have two hundred and sixteen. I have no idea what happened to the others. I'm reworking the chart as we go. This is, this is guano, some of them don't even know each other . . ."

"There is no time to look for the missing ones, it's going to blow again soon . . ."

"I plucking know!" he shouted. "At least you found Veruma—the seven of us are here—"

"About Veruma—" I was about to say reasonably, *I'm accepting your suggestion to connect with Somay instead,* but what came out of my mouth was, "Veruma doesn't like me right now, and if she needs to like me to connect with me, we have a problem."

"Oh, pluck it, Ranra, just take Somay, what's one more substitution in the chart?" He was agitated, in a bad way. This wasn't how it was supposed to go. If I swapped Veruma with Somay after talking to her, I'd be punishing her for being upset with me. I'd be making this worse, and I did not want that.

"Let me talk to her again," I said. Ulár hadn't slept much. We both were high-strung from a heady mix of deep concentration and exhaustion, but we would push through. Ulár, of all people, understood about emergencies, and didn't need his feelings tended when things were exploding, and thank Bird for that. We *would* do this.

"Wait for me, please." I was proud of myself to have remembered to add a please, but Ulár never seemed to be bothered by my domineering ways. He always argued right back and just as aggressively. I found that restful, especially now.

Ulár was not the problem. Veruma was.

I found her standing with the other erams, talking quietly with Lilún. "Veruma, can I have a few words?"

"Sure." She came after me, just a few steps away. There wasn't much privacy to be had in the crowded main courtyard, under the ashen, shuddering sky. "What is it?"

"Veruma, listen, the three connections I will form will filter everybody else's power through these three people's configurations, if I understand Ulár's theories correctly. These three people especially need to have deep friendship, deep trust. I chose you, but I know we are having a rough time if it, so—if you don't want to connect with me, we can swap."

"You do not trust me," Veruma said harshly.

"I trust you with my life," I said. "I would rather have you, but I accept it if you'd rather swap."

Veruma clenched her fists. "I do not want to be chosen out of pity."

Through my connection to the star, I felt the next eruption rise in my throat like bile. "Duck for cover!" I yelled as the sky exploded. Gusts of wind carried debris, and ash obscured the sky. Belatedly, the shrill sounds of the shofar longhorn drifted from the mountain, Somay's warning system rendered utterly redundant now that we could both hear and see the eruption. I just hoped that whoever Somay had positioned there was safe.

Veruma didn't duck. She just stood there, staring at me, ignoring all danger. I unbent from where I'd ducked, and stared back. Veruma's face was streaked with ash and defiant; her eyes shone with anger and more than a little self-loathing. By Bird, she was magnificent. Somay . . . I respected Somay, but they never stood up to me. And sure, Veruma needed her feelings tended when things were exploding, but I owed her that.

I took a step toward her, extended my hands. She ignored them. I said, "I do not pity you."

"No? My weak configuration—everybody knows that I, I, I cannot advance beyond where I'm at, I'm barely holding the Princely Angle!"

"Veruma, please. I chose you. It was my decision, to connect to the three people closest to me, not the three strongest people. I chose you, Erígra, and Ulár. I don't care if you aren't the strongest. I love you. You are my friend. We—we gift each other everything."

"What?" Veruma said, her voice hoarse.

"It's . . . something Dorod told Erígra. And Erígra told me. And I am telling you. It is true. This—this is us, this is the isles. It matters more than power." I wasn't actually sure I was right. But I chose that. I chose her.

She stood there, still unconvinced. And I realized something. That apology I owed her since she came for me after my near-death at the foot of Semberí's hill, I still owed it. So I made it. "I am sorry I treated you so badly. I am sorry I took you for granted. I am sorry I could not be a better friend to you. If you choose to swap, I will not fault you. I will not love you less."

Veruma inhaled through clenched teeth. Her eyes glistened. "Do you want me to swap? Somay *is* stronger. I will not fault you either."

I inhaled, too. This was the moment of our truth. "I don't want you to swap."

"Then I will support you," said Veruma. "To the end of the world, and beyond."

"And I, you." This, too, had been a thing we said.

Our structure clarified and the worst of the wind being over, we returned to our places in the courtyard. I climbed on a toppled stone. Veruma, Lilún, and Ulár surrounded me. My stomach churned, and I was glad that I had not eaten. Around me, the city I loved lay in ruins. It was salvageable—all salvageable—if only I could succeed.

"We are beginning," I called out. "Those assembled here, the powerful named strong summoned and ready to work together, even at a short notice, with little preparation, because preparation is dangerous—I give my respect and my admiration, my love and my gratitude to you, to all of us, to this community, this city splendid under Bird's wings, coming together to heal our star. We will only get this one chance, and we will give it our all—archipelago-style—"

The people cheered, and I continued.

"On my command, Ulár will begin calling out your names and the syllable counts one by one. When he calls your name and the syllable count of the deepname you are extending, you will connect with your counterpart through that deepname. It will take time, but this will be the least confusing way forward. Once the connection is formed, you must hold it, and keep holding it while others are connecting."

I stopped for their nods and yelled acknowledgments. "We will connect from outward in, from the longest deepnames to the shortest. Once the structure is complete, these three erams will then connect to me, and I will then draw on our collective power. I seek this power not for myself, not for any glory or pride, but as the one sent forth by the community to represent us all . . . I will not misuse the power given to me by all of you, this I swear on the goddess's wing, I will attempt to do what must be done, to chart the best path forward, to do the work, to heal the star, to repair the world . . . Thank you for your trust."

By the time I was done, the mood turned somber. Few people clapped or cheered, but that was fine, too. Ulár unrolled the last, very last, final, absolutely final version of his chart, black and red with numerous corrections. In a clear voice, he called out, "Marev Nafadli and Sedar

Teuma, three syllable! Oshera Gala and Panúr Nedaar, three syllable!"

I stood on my stone and watched the people connect. This was hard, laborious, and many times Ulár had to run into the crowd to coach a pair of named strong. A few people lost their connections, and had to reform them. The sun was traveling in the sky, its journey barely seen through the thick, blanketing clouds. I squeezed Veruma's shoulder, and Lilún's. I had gleaned something from my talks with Lilún and the healing books we studied in last few days, and I had a plan, and I had my people around me. This was good, I repeated to myself. This was good.

Finally, Ulár stopped calling out names. Only the four of us remained.

Veruma and I extended our two-syllables, and connected. I felt her mood clearly now. Worried, and determined, a bit proud. She didn't feel angry.

I understood now why the Royal House was the best for rulers. The two-syllable stabilized the configuration, but it also allowed me to connect to my people. In the structure we made, the longest and weakest deepname needed to connect first. The Warlord's Triangle, technically the strongest configuration in existence, was a closed system. Three single-syllables. It would not allow me to connect to anyone. I had been right to reject it.

Lilún reached to me next, in a wave of tenderness, warmth, and precision. I would never tire of connecting with them, the joy of our discovery, our trust. I loved them so much, and by Bird, I would win for us more time. I smiled at them, and they smiled back, but I couldn't dwell on it, because Ulár tapped me impatiently on the shoulder. His mind was angular, and as quick as my own, and the connection with him felt heaviest. He was a three-named strong, the only one of my inner circle, and he brought with him twice the connections that Lilún and Veruma were bringing. This felt lopsided, unbalanced. It would have been better, perhaps, to choose all three-named strong, or all two-named strong, but there was no redoing this now. I frowned, and the mountain rumbled in the distance. *Now, Ranra, now, now or never,* I told myself.

"We begin!" I yelled, my stomach churning, and almost immediately I pulled on my connection to Veruma, Lilún, and Ulár, reaching through them to all their connections, pulling gently but inexorably through them, through this living net we'd made of each other.

Ulár's connection to me flowed steadily, broadly almost, flooding me with power. Lilún's was like a clear, joyful river, not as plentiful as Ulár's, but wonderful in feel. Veruma's flowed with the goodness of her, the hard work she put into everything she did, but the stream of power emerged through her with an effort. The unbalanced effect of this power was hard, but I managed to grasp it and pull, and pull, and pull, through my dearest ones, from the power of my people, my city, my isles, until I felt myself soaring.

In my vision, I was a bird. Not a crow, but a cormorant, a diving bird, enormous, ascending into the ashen and darkening sky, laboriously beating its wings. Higher and higher, lifted up by the power of all of us, drawn endlessly, intensifying until I could see no sky, feel no warmth and no cold. The whole world filled up with the power of song, a single, long-drawn note that rose as I rose, clear-pitched like the call of the ancient shofar long-horn being blown from the mountain, not useless now, but guiding me with all its might, unerring, unending.

Then, just as abruptly, the sound came to an end. I hung in the air overlooking the island of Geu. Mother Mountain, spitting flame, a rivulet of red running down its slope. Burning pines. My city in ruins. My people, assembled resolutely around my physical shape. Below me, the sea. Deep in the wave, the sputtering, splintering blue of my star.

The moment of stillness broke, and I was diving, plummeting through the air. My wings were closed, my whole being attuned to the new longhorn sound of my dive. I was piercing the air, speeding faster and faster toward the heart of the wave.

Impact. Then silence, as the waters parted around my cormorant body. I dove deeper and deeper toward my star. I was enormous with power and resolute and beautiful to myself and afraid, deep inside so afraid, but I drew and drew on the power of my people, the un-ending wave of it, aware now of all the many imper-fections, people dropping out of connections, people fainting, others stepping in—the single-named strong, those waiting around us—to give of themselves where others could not. Through all this, the mighty river which was Ulár flowed unconquered through me, and Lilún's smaller, livelier river came easily, gently, up-holding me. Veruma struggled, overwhelmed, but yet she held on, and her struggles distracted me for a moment before I regained my grip on my vision.

I was facing the star, the enormous, agitated ball of blue floating underneath the islands. I was smaller than the star still, but not as small as during my first attempts. This was good. The power of my people was enough. This was good, I repeated to myself. I could do this.

I reached toward the star, and aligned myself to it. My talks with Lilún, and the healing books I read quickly, and my own insights—gleaned from the connection and my previous attempts—all told me I had to create a resonance, a kind of amplitude of magic gently rotating, moving, attuning the star to me.

I focused my will and my mind, and began. Push and pull. Push and pull. Push and pull. Push and pull.

The star's sputtering was growing less agitated. I could feel it—this was working—I just had to continue—

I am elsewhere. In the enormous white city of chiseled lions and piers and tall towers of spun glass. I am small, on the ground. I am running and running as explosions rattle the city, demolishing towers, raining glass on the ground, cleaving sculptures in two. My arms fill with hundreds of tiny, jagged cuts, but I run still. I run.

A person in a billowing blue dress stands on a fallen stone lion. The person is tall and determined. I don't know how this world is arranged, but they look like a woman to me, or perhaps an ichidi with long, unbraided hair. Woman, I guess. All around her are people, connecting to each other, connecting to her just as my people connected to me. More and more people are connecting now, many more than I've ever imagined, uncounted thousands of them as fire tears apart the sky.

The woman screams at them, urges them, but there is no time left. I see them dying, falling onto the cracking and scalded earth. More people run to take their place. The woman draws on them, draws them all in, the living and the dead, as a humongous crack runs through the city, through buildings, and they crumble. This world has moments left, I know. The people give of themselves to the woman as they die. I do not know if they die, or if she kills them. They give willingly, like dying people would give their souls willingly to Bird, but she is no Bird. She is human, and as she receives them she cries out in denial, in anguish, in anger, for all those she drew on are powerful adults, and there are no children among them. No children even hope to be saved.

She screams now, despair swallowing her, but she is still defiant. She pulls, and all her people die, her city is dying around her, the whole world is breaking, no longer white but ashen, burnt, besmirched with corrosion and fire and death, but she is transcendent, having collected the freely given souls of her people. Now she is no longer human—her shape is circular now, dense with soul-deepnames, short ones in the middle, longer ones on the edges. She has acquired the color of storm that grows vaster as more and more people fling themselves into her ever-expanding star shape. She holds on to it, to herself, as her world is ending. Darkness devours all except her, a spitting, sputtering, weeping ball of sea-blue.

And then I hear Bird's wings.

What are the twelve stars? Who are the twelve stars?

The stars are travelers, each from a different world . . .

I am flung out of my vision-within-the-vision, but I am still in the sea, still facing the star as it sputters and spins and cries. The amplitude I had created is shattered. The star spins, agitated, angry, despairing, DESPAIR-ING. I can redo this—try again— I need to calm her—and I tug and tug and tug on my connections, but they have diminished now—more people fell there, in the courtyard, by my slumping physical body. I know at this moment that I cannot heal her. Even if I can reach her, I don't have enough power. Not anymore. I could have succeeded if I knew all this earlier, touched her earlier, came to her gently as a friend comes, came to understand her pain, but there was no *time*. And now she is more despairing than ever, she is spinning out of control, out of care, out of help.

But something else presents itself.

I, too, could.

I could, right now, still, pull on the souls of my people, those living and newly dead by my side. I would take them into me, endlessly, ravenously, eagerly, regretfully, triumphantly. I too could expand and become huge with souls, I could expand and pull on my connection to my star, pull and pull and pull until I devour her too, and all the souls she'd saved. My own people and her people I would absorb and become the Resolute Star, the star of my will, a star that expanded out of the vast power of both people and stars, the Star which is not quiet but which is determined in her survival. Most of these named strong would die, and so would many others in Gelle-Geu, and the Sputtering Star would die, but the isles would be saved, and some of our children would be saved, and we would eventually rebuild, and I, I would live like this underwave, and I would keep them in peace and prosperity forever. Lilún—Lilún would be my first starkeeper—

My connection to the Sputtering Star felt wounded. The star was screaming, resisting —not nearly strong enough to compete with my will—I would absorb her now for my people . . . The star screamed endlessly, fearfully, like a sleeper lost in the nightmare, and I was that nightmare.

I fought myself. No. No. No.

Somebody touched my shoulder. There, in the courtyard. Lilún.

No. I could not do this, no matter the cost. This was wrong. My people did not give their consent. Nor this star. My people consented to aid me in the healing of the star, they wanted me to be their representative, the leader of their congregation, the one to carry their offering, not the hoarder of their souls, not a nightmare devourer of them—

Not their murderer.

I will not misuse the power given to me by all of us, this I swear on the goddess's wing, only to do what must be done, to take the best path forward . . . even if I cannot repair the world . . .

I pulled away from the Sputtering Star. Enormous pain flooded me as the tether that anchored me to my star was severed, and in the last of my vision, the star thrashed in the wave, in pure despair of her nightmares, flinging herself against the islands, against the root of the mountain.

This was the end.

I screamed, gulping water. I was drowning, deep in the sea.

No. No. This was real, but I was also elsewhere. Choking, I yanked myself out of my vision. Into a different one.

In that vision I saw lava, pouring out of the Mother Mountain unbalanced by the star, the star unbalanced even more by my actions. A tide of fire sweeping through Gelle-Geu, sweeping through the harbor, devouring Dorod's ships before they could launch. And then, darkness.

Lilún

With an anguished wail, the structure fell apart. The wail was coming out of my own mouth, and I wasn't the only one screaming. All around us, I heard cries and gasps. I wasn't powerful enough to see Bird as she came for the souls of the newly dead, but I saw Ulár's eyes dart to and fro as he tracked the goddess collecting our fallen friends. Ranra swayed on her stone, and I grabbed her, steadied her. She was alive, at least. Her eyes were closed.

Before I could do anything, she peeled her blood-shot eyes open. She said, "The mountain is about to erupt. Lava is all I see. It will reach here too soon for the ships."

"What happened with our work?" Somay asked. "Healing the star?"

"We failed," croaked Ranra. "I failed. We must go Dorod's way now, if we still can."

"Are you sure that we failed? I thought the structure worked," said Ulár, at the same time as Veruma asked, "Was it because of me?"

Ranra pressed her hands to her ears. She said, "Yes, I'm sure, no, Veruma, it wasn't because of you, it's the structure itself—this way—"

"The structure worked," Ulár insisted.

"Yes, but without knowing—to heal, you must first understand—and with a great intricacy—pluck it, I unbalanced the star even more, I unbalanced every-thing—"

An explosion rocked the mountain, and it crowned itself in brilliant fire.

"We must win more time." Ranra straightened her-self. "The people on the outer islands—Agara, Meh-mey, Terreo—they know the plan, but we need to signal them."

She squared her shoulders. Yelled at us. "Erams, get your people—get my people too, get the children, all the children you can find, get named strong of sig-nificant ability, if any are still left, to help us steer the ships—Penár and Bodavár to connect with the outer islands, they have a bit more time—go, go, go—I must get to the Mother Mountain."

"You've done so much, but this is wrong," Somay said

passionately. "The ships idea was good to briefly discuss, but we cannot—there aren't enough ships—this cannot be the only way. The working felt good—it might not be the end, we could still endure here . . ."

Ranra spoke forcefully. "Do as I say now. Go, go, go. Get the children, get the powerful adults, connect with Dorod, you know your assigned ship, GO."

She did not wait for an answer, just pushed everybody out of her way and broke into a wobbly, labored run, and this time I caught up with her easily. "I am with you."

"Pluck you, Lilún, get your people and get them to your ship—"

"You haven't made me eram, have you forgotten? Ranra, Ulár, Veruma, Somay, Bodavár, Penár, Dorod. The seven erams, I'm not one of them, I know nothing about either ships or people . . ." I was becoming winded as Ranra's steps lengthened.

"Then I made a mistake. What's another mistake after all this, eh?" She was running now.

"You lay still for hours, that time at the foot of Semberí's hill, but now you led a much bigger working and yet you are running," I huffed by her side.

"Didn't have enough power. Have enough power now."

She would not tell me more about our great work, what she saw there at the very end. I saw glimpses of it, more than enough. A whole world, ending. The star—the star had once been someone like Ranra. Her people's savior. Her people's grave. "Ranra, I want to understand . . ."

"I failed, Lilún, what's there to understand? The star is thrashing under the wave. It is throwing itself against the roots of the islands. It is not asleep anymore, it is aware and remembering, and it is remembering horrors. I no longer even have the connection. Its only connection is to the mountain. You want me to stop and discuss this? I can't."

"What are you going to do once we reach the mountain?" I asked her.

"Plead."

We reached the ashen, smoking, blackened slopes of the mountain. Ranra told me she knew many running paths up the mountain, but boulders had rained down from above, blocking all easy ways up. Ranra did not stop. Finding her way among the stones, she climbed like a woman desperate, possessed. It was hard to breathe here, and I begged Ranra to stop, or at least to slow down, but she ignored me. Up she climbed, and I followed her, straining. She knew the mountain well, but I doubted there was anything familiar here now.

At last, we reached a wide, charred ledge. Once a pine tree grew here. Only its scorched ghost remained now.

Here, Ranra stopped, and tilted her head up toward the angry, flaming peak, and yelled, "Mother Mountain!!" Her voice echoed, a hollow sound. "Please, Mother!"

I was not sure what Ranra was doing, or why, or even if she had still the full grip of her senses. Ranra paid me and my worries no heed.

She pulled on her deepnames, and they felt pain-

ful to me, overworked and overused, but still she constructed of them a triangle, and amplified by its power,
she yelled again, "Mother Mountain!" And again, her
voice echoed, starker and deeper than before.

I could not imagine activating my own deepnames
after the work we've just done, but Ranra's configuration held. And perhaps I, too, was addled from our
exertion and our failure, but it felt like the mountain
was listening.

"Mother, please. Please, Mother, down below—in the
city, my people are trying to get to the ships. I can feel
the lava rising in you, see the breath of ash and smoke,
and I believe you are still connected to the star. She is
tugging at you, disturbing you. I have failed her, I'm
sorry, and I have failed you too, but you are my mother,
I come to you in my hour of need, please, hold your
fire for a mere few hours, let your children get into the
ships, leave safely." Ranra spun her tired, weakened
configuration above her head, speaking on and on and
on. "Just a few more hours, Mother—"

I felt it then, a connection that was raw and vulnerable and real, between Ranra and the mountain. A connection like the one she'd once shared with the star. I
could see it spinning out, an offering, a plea.

The mountain rumbled, a low, terrible sound. The
mountain was refusing. No—no, something else. The
mountain could not. The mountain needed—

I narrowed my eyes and saw a brief vision—not
Ranra's, my own. The mountain slopes in autumn,
warm and welcoming. Between the pines, two brown
bears were ambling amiably. The air was sweet with

honey and golden light. The mountain was mother, and father too.

I wished I had come here earlier, when the pines were still tall and splendid enough to build ships, not charred ghosts amid the devastation. The mountain was now connected to the despairing, dying star. The tether between them was painfully frayed. I felt the rumble intensify, and bile rose in my throat.

"Mother—please listen to me—even for a few hours—a mere few hours!" Ranra shouted. "You need— you need—I do not have the power you need—" She turned to me, her eyes bloodshot and wild. "Lilún— help me. Can you . . . ?"

I wanted to do this. With all my being I wanted to help. I tried and tried to summon my deepnames, but I could not. After our big working, my mind felt completely burned out. My mouth opened, but I could not say anything. Not to apologize, not to explain. Ranra's deepnames were still engaged. She was that strong-willed, that resolute. That far gone.

"So be it. So be it!" Ranra did not look well as she clutched her hair and tore a large clump of it out, and I saw—I saw the triangle of magic above her head wobble.

The mountain shook violently now, spewing clouds of ash, and Ranra screamed and screamed as she directed the power of her two single-syllables upon her weaker, longer two-syllable. The two-syllable sputtered, then winked out. Ranra sobbed, and I took a step toward her, but she held me at bay with an imperious gesture of her hand.

Where the two-syllable deepname had just winked

out in her mind, a stronger, shorter deepname flared to life.

I had only read of such things, but my lover had broken her mind, shortened her two-syllable into a single-syllable. She now wielded the Warlord's Triangle, the most powerful, ruthless, and destructive configuration of them all. I did not know a single person in the isles who wielded it. We were not a warlike people.

Ranra yelled like a desperate woman rushing forward with a knife. She reformed her configuration into a sharp, immensely potent triangle, which she spun and directed upon the mountain, constructing from it a grid. A stricture. A bondage. She flung that at the mountain, at the painful, ragged tether that connected the mountain to the star, strengthening it. Stabilizing it. Constricting it.

"This will hold!" Ranra screamed. "It will hold!"

A powerful reverberation shook the slope, and stones rattled under our feet. From above, a long, low whistle erupted, then weakened.

Silence.

Ranra's eyes were closed.

She toppled, as if in a dream, backwards from the ledge which held us, falling into the nothingness of air.

With all my might and unthinking, I twisted and jumped, threw my hands out as if I was daring and well-trained, which I wasn't. I was going to miss. No—Ranra meant so much to me, and I'd sworn to support her, and the world was ending, so what would it matter if I died? I would dive after her, even from the mountain, to catch her and bring her home.

In that endless, brief, brilliant moment, my body and my self aligned. My screaming mind exuded the deep-names it had refused me before. They twisted painfully, forming an angle, lending me strength and agility beyond anything I knew.

I grabbed her korob. Then her wrist. Pulled her out.

ᗐARIATION THE ᖴIFTH:
ZÚR

I carry my world

Ranra

I was only dimly aware of Lilún, their body supporting mine, my right arm over their shoulders. I saw the world blurred, through my slitted eyes. Semidarkness, and dust in the air.

We were walking somewhere. On a road made of stones. It did not matter.

I had failed.

My connection to the star had been severed, but I felt her dying throes in my bones. My head felt much like the dying star, all throbbing and pain. Somay thought we shouldn't rush. That it wouldn't be this bad. Well, pluck Somay.

If I had connected with Somay, not Veruma, would I have been successful? Veruma thought so. Her face had said it all, stricken and guilty. But I knew it would have been worse.

How worse?

I needed to think this through, but my head was on fire. I'd done something to myself up there, on the slopes of Mother Mountain.

Lilún stumbled, and I swayed against them. They righted themself. Their configuration was engaged, and the warmth of it supported my weight. My thoughts darted—like a deep, red-hot poker of pain just above my right eye. We were going somewhere. It didn't matter.

Where was I? Veruma. Veruma thought she'd failed me, failed the whole enterprise. But if I had Somay, who did not love me, and who was more powerful, I would have been able to tap into their colder, vaster power. I would have had even less love to offer the star. I would have destroyed it—not over hours, like now, but all at once, and everything would have ended. Not choosing Somay had brought us something—a bit of time. But this failure was mine alone.

To heal, you must first understand what hurts. To heal, you must first become trusted.

Push and pull, Lilún had said, but their touch was light. Mine wasn't.

I couldn't have healed the star, not the way I approached this. This wasn't just about simple consent—I had to get to know her first, to understand her. I needed a gentler hand. Nothing else would have worked. I understood that now. What I'd done was powerful, but it reawakened the star's pain and added to it, and instead of healing, I unbalanced her beyond all healing.

Lilún—Lilún knew instinctively what would have worked, but they had recoiled from that work. Semberí thought Lilún was the one, and they could have been, but it was all too much for them. Who could blame them? Lilún did not love the star. They loved the quince

in the grove, and clear nights, and poetry. Lilún, perhaps, loved me.

Perhaps this was even simpler. Lilún was not used to
carrying pain in their heart every day, like I did. I could
carry the pain, but I did not have the gentleness.

I had failed to understand. I had failed to lead. I
failed, I failed, I failed.

What right did any of them have to love me? To support me?

I pulled away from Lilún and swayed on my feet.
Pried open my eyes. The shrill, rumbling sounds filled
the air, the screeching of birds, the desperate echoing
winds.

"Where are we going?" I muttered.

"You're back! Praise Bird!" Lilún's voice was so full of
relief and warmth that I wanted to punch them. "We're
trying to make it to Geu Harbor . . . Not far now."

I peered ahead, where the road was covered with debris. The earth kept shaking. There was nothing ahead
of us that I could see.

"What happened?" My head throbbed.

They said, "You stopped the mountain. Bought us
time. With luck, many of our people have escaped, and
a ship might still be waiting for us."

I swallowed. Remembering. I chained my own
Mother. I thought that she wanted—she asked for—
but now I wasn't sure. Could she free herself from her
bond if she wanted to? Maybe. My head felt like it was
bursting.

"You go. Just let me plucking lie down and die. I
failed, Lilún . . ."

"I don't care," they said fiercely. "You did not fail me. You led us when everybody else gave up or pretended everything was fine, or waited, Bird knows for what. Yes, our way didn't work—"

"Our way was dangerous—more dangerous than you know—"

"I saw some of it," they said.

"It must never be attempted again."

"If you say so . . ."

"We failed—this is not a peaceful structure, Lilún. This structure kills. This structure takes and takes from everyone to give it to one person. It puts too much strain on the people, people died when I pulled on them, and it fed me and made me crave more—and all I could have accomplished with this power was to kill everyone who trusted me, devour them and the star, become a star myself, circling ravenously under-wave like a shark that eats its own kind, desiring only to devour. This must never be attempted again."

"Then tell this to our people," Lilún said passionately. "Share your knowledge, teach us."

"Our people are no more," I said hoarsely. "I led them to ruin."

"Dorod told me this before we began," said Lilún, "that our culture must survive. Not many cultures in this world are like ours. Laaguti escaped here, and so did others. Their stories survive in our hearts, their words survive in our language. They came here because of us. Who we are is important, is precious, is rare. Each one of us is the whole of our people, carrying all our love and our failures and our histories in our bones, and unless we all perish, nobody and nothing can take that away. Even if Gelle-Geu and all of our friends and family are gone, there's still the two of us. We are the fruit of the quince tree that will birth the grove."

I swallowed the lump in my throat. Tried to hide behind bluster. "Dorod told you all of this? Because I don't think they were ever this poetic."

"Maybe they did. I don't remember exactly."

Despite myself, I took a step forward. My mind, aching with my new powertaking, refused to settle when I tried to activate my deepnames. The more I tried, the more it felt like I was tearing my own head up with my fingers-turned-claws. Still, I tried again and again, walking forward with ever-lengthening steps.

My deepnames activated at last: first the original, achy one-syllable deepnames, then the new one. The new deepname was agonizing to hold. My old configuration did not hurt, but this one was an iron stake of headache in my mind, constant, throbbing. And it was potent. Red with blood and so, so powerful. I gritted my teeth and made a triangle.

My magical senses, dulled by exertion and injury, flared to life, bringing clarity. From afar, amid the darkness and rubble of Gelle-Geu, I saw bird shapes flicker in and out of the air, too large to be real birds. My people were dying, and the goddess was coming for them. Two, three, four. We had more people than that.

"I do not believe everybody is gone," I said. "We must help the survivors."

"Yes."

My Warlord's Triangle, held with great difficulty at

first, invigorated me. Power streamed from my mind into my limbs, sweeping away aches and pains, pumping blood into every sinew and bone. I had never felt so good. So potent. So full. The headache was more intense now, but I grasped my configuration, grasped even the headache. All this pain was mine, and I fed on it.

By the time we reached what had once been Gelle-Geu, I was running again.

The city lay in ruins. We rushed past the crumbled houses, the besmirched beauty of Gelle-Geu, its lost people. I couldn't stop to honor the dead I saw. Somebody had to have been alive, somebody whom my power would serve. When the sea view unfolded itself, I saw the ships that had sailed, barely out of the harbor, struggling mightily on turbulent waters. I saw people on the decks, powerful named strong with their magic activated, attempting to pacify the wave. Many smaller boats were dancing on the water. In the harbor, two ships still remained. The new, unpainted one— Dorod's— and the one they'd assigned to me. There was a desperate crowd in the harbor, grownups and children, some screaming and others silent. All parted way for me.

Dorod came forward, their face lined with care. They looked older now, but still as resolute. Behind them I saw a few of the people assigned to my own ship, my trusted companions and helpers, my librarian—but none of the other erams were there. With any luck, they would be with their ships.

"I am glad to see you both alive," said Dorod gravely.

"Ranra stopped the mountain from erupting," Lilún said. "We have—"

I interrupted them. "How are we faring?"

"It's not safe to sail," said Dorod. "But we have no other choice. There are enough three-named strong to pacify the sea momentarily, but the turbulence—"

"We'll make it," I said, hoarsely. What did it matter, one more attempt, one more failure? What did it matter if I lied? I had never lied before, but such matters seemed meaningless now. My mind felt different. But this was better. With the Warlord's Triangle, I could no longer form the big structure, could no longer be tempted to devour anyone. I was safe.

"How many have we managed to fit?"

Dorod said, "Almost everyone, actually. Many people refused to set sail. While you were gone, I persuaded as many as I could, but many more are hiding in what remains of their homes, or with friends, cursing you—I am sorry—saying you lost it like your mother, or simply believing the mountain would calm down and the weather would clear."

We looked to each other, grim. There was no time and no reason to try to persuade more people. There was no room.

"Forgive me asking," I said. "But I have been wondering why Terein never ordered a whole fleet of ships to be built, to save everyone, or at least most of us. Why would he refuse?"

"It took him a while. He, too, studied the star. In the end, he believed that no ship could survive the star's dissolution."

I grumbled, "He could send people elsewhere, see if we could find a place to settle."

"Oh, he raised it at council once. People laughed him out of the room—Terein the Despairing, Terein the Fearful. This was a year or two before you joined the council. Some of these people you know. Most of the others have since retired. No, not Veruma," Dorod said, seeing my expression. "But they mocked Terein."

I scowled. "He did not argue back?"

"No. He never mentioned it again, and wouldn't look at a star chart after that. I barely convinced him to let me build these ships. 'You would have no workers,' he told me. 'They think it's nonsense.' I said I would build them as tradeships."

I wished I'd known all this, I wished I could've talked to Terein, without judgement, with patience. But if I had been in that room, I would have said the same thing that I said—that we had an obligation to fix, not to run away from our land on a fear that things would go wrong.

Without speaking, Dorod grasped my right arm, and I, theirs.

I said, "I will lead us out of here, Dorod."

They nodded gravely. "Yes."

"But I see children still on the shore . . . Is there nothing we can discard?"

Dorod's ship was already full to capacity. The people assigned to my ship spoke up about the precious pieces of art and the books from the Keeper's library, all our history and our splendor and our learning. I stared them down. "Discard everything but the immediate supplies."

"But, Ranra . . ." they protested.

"Every child here will make it. Every. Child. Get to it."

"Did you load any quince?" said Lilún to Dorod.

"We have quince wine on board." Dorod looked perplexed.

"No . . . the fruit . . ."

"Shut up, everyone," I bellowed. "Throw it all away. Pour the plucking wine out, too."

"Ranra, I'm going," said Lilún. "A piece of fruit won't take any room. I will put it in my pocket. I will put it in my mouth. Destroy everything else, but the quince is the symbol of our people."

Lilún was backing away from me. I lurched forward to grab them, but they jumped away. "I do not give my consent to be stopped. I am going."

"I can't wait for you," I yelled after them. "You told me yourself that people were more important than things—"

But Lilún was already running.

Lilún

Once upon a time I was an ichidi who woke up each morning in my own bed, which my fathers had painted with little silver fish. I would dress and go out, sometimes with my spade and my bucket and shears, sometimes empty-handed, and walk to the grove. Over and over, I refused my ancestor's ghost, but came back for their company and their stories. I breathed in the awakening sea, and touched the gentle bark of the quince trees. It was a quiet life, translucent and slow, with a layer of sadness over the sweet, complex odor of the quince. I had been almost content—and the yearnings and moves of my soul I'd shaped into poetry. Making poems had felt as natural as exhaling. Now, I could not imagine writing again.

The hill was there—visible, waiting for me, but when I climbed up, I found the grove destroyed. Broken branches and splintered trunks littered the ground. I saw fruit, still mostly young and unripe, on the dark, tortured ground at my feet.

I knelt there at the grove. The earth was shaking, the tremors stronger and stronger. This would be the last time, I knew, the last time I touched my fingers to this wet, generous soil, the last time I breathed this air. My hand, unbidden, wrapped around a quince. My mouth shaped a name. "Semberí."

"I made a terrible mistake." Semberí's voice, behind me. So bitter. "I told you there still was a year, until a thousand years will have passed. I counted them from the Birdcoming."

I did not even turn, but relief swept through me, to find them—not alive, but around.

"Come with me," I pleaded with them. "You weigh nothing. I'll carry you."

They ignored me. "I counted a thousand years since

my own hurt. I blamed the Orphan Star's influence, but I—I miscounted."

Finally, I attended to their words. "Yes?"

"When you made your big construct and Ranra"—they snarled her name. Tried again. "When Ranra touched the star, I saw . . ."

There was a long pause. I thought Semberí would leave, like they often did when they did not care to continue, but the ghost simply floated around me, then crouched by my side. Their form, tattered and insubstantial, undulated in front of me. Their eyes were vortices of blue, wavering and shimmering. If they weren't a ghost, I would think they were crying.

"It wasn't a thousand years since the Birdcoming. Not a thousand years since the Orphan Star's company. It was a thousand years counted from this disaster we'd seen. I had carried her pain, but I thought—" Semberí swirled around feebly. "I should have counted from her death. From the death of her world. That happened before the Birdcoming, before the star even hung on Bird's tail. I was too full of myself."

"A year wouldn't have mattered," I said. But I wasn't sure. When I'd touched the star, that time with Ulár and Somay, I'd sensed I could have helped if I had been willing to face the despair that she carried. But I wasn't. I thought I'd explained the healing cadence to Ranra, and she gave it her best, but it did not work out in the end. Perhaps we needed to work together, the two of us. It was too late for that now.

"You told me not to refuse my destiny," I said. "I failed."

They swirled around, the circles of emptiness increased in their body, devouring them from within. "I should have revealed the hill earlier. A year was not enough for you. You needed many years—a lifetime of years—lifetimes many of us had, and none of us figured it out . . . But Ranra, Ranra was never suited for this. She sped up the dissolution—shortened what little time we still had—and you were not strong enough on your own."

"Pluck you." I sounded like Ranra now. "Yes, I wish I could have been braver, stronger. I needed more time, and perhaps after a lifetime I still wouldn't have been ready. You had a thousand years—what have you done with them? Haunted this hill, guarded these trees, judged every starkeeper and every would-be starkeeper?"

Semberí said, "What did I *do*? I convinced the star to sleep. She slept so fitfully, but I tethered her to the mountain to stabilize her. I gave us almost a thousand years . . ."

"She didn't need to be bound, Semberí, she needed a healer. Perhaps that had to be me, or you, or Terein, or Dorod, or a hundred others before my time, but Ranra was the one who took it on. Don't you see, Semberí, how hard she worked—with all her strength, her conviction, her willingness to shoulder the pain—and she could have succeeded. She did everything she could, Semberí, she did more than anyone, and certainly more than you!"

They floated up with a great whoosh of air, and I was sure they were gone now. I put the fruit into my pocket and stood up. Saw that they were still there, their tattered back turned to me.

"What are you doing here?" the ghost asked.

I said, "I came for you."

"No, the fruit."

"I am taking a quince. I thought you might put it into my pocket yourself, but this will have to serve."

Semberí flew toward me. The wind gusted now, blowing Semberí's form to and fro. In the middle of their face, where their eyes and nose would have been, was a vortex. Their mouth of air still moved. Their voice sounded incredulous. "You want me to put a seed into your pocket?"

"I was hoping you would," I said. "A promise of hope for our children, if any survive. A new story, even if we do not understand it yet."

"Wait here!" the ghost suddenly screamed.

"What?"

"Wait here—if you ever cared for me, wait here!" Semberí's spirit whirled up, flowed into a shape of a bird. It was a marsh bird—a small white egret with a sharp, long beak and strong, gray-tipped wings that now beat the air as the ghost bird rose up and up, away from the hill, over the turbulent sea where six grand ships and many lesser ones now struggled with the violent currents, drifting farther and farther away.

Higher and higher the white egret rose, then plummeted down like an arrow. I could not see when it hit the water.

Six tradeships, and a flock of other, smaller ones. Two great ones had launched from Agara and Mehmey, and I hoped that my fathers were aboard. But there was another ship still not on the water.

Someone was waiting for me. Was it so? My heart lurched with hope.

The quince was in my pocket. I quickly bent over, and found another one. Two gave us more hope than one, but this would need to be enough—if Ranra still waited for me, she was risking so much, she was risking the children—I had to go—

Wait here, if you ever cared for me. Semberí or Ranra? Ranra or Semberí?

Both. I choose both.

The sea boiled, a loud, belching, quaking sound. A giant bell of explosion came from the mountain, and a crown of fire sprouted from it. An explosion, and the top of the mountain lifted up, and lava poured down the slopes toward Gelle-Geu. We were done for. I needed—I needed—

From below, I heard a voice carrying toward me, Ranra's cry amplified by her powerful deepnames. "Lilún!!! 'Lilúúúúúúún!!!!! Lilúúúúúúúúúúúúúún!!!"

And an enormous white egret arose from the turbulent sea, a ghost bird speeding up and up and up from the water toward the hill, coming here with a wild, desperate cry of its own. "Erígra!!!!!"

The egret was beating its wings, coming closer, and I saw that it had a new blue heart—no, no, the bird was hollow in the middle, where a large jewel of blue purer than the purest azure hung suspended on nothing, held tenderly by the emptied-out body of the ghost bird. It flew up the hill, each movement of its wings so slow and so difficult, and I reached—I stretched my hands up and out toward it, like the guardians of old had reached up toward Bird. My vision was blurring, and my heart, like a house locked all my life, was opening now, opening toward the vision of the blue jewel—our dying star's purest, most tender essence. The seed.

"I am here!" I shouted, to Semberí, to myself, to the goddess Bird. "I am here! I am here!!!!"

Behind Semberí's egret I saw, for the moment, the spread of other, greater wings, their brilliance filling the sky. The egret screamed, its voice like a bell that shook my bones, "Begin again!"

The seed detached from the ghost egret's swirling body, and arcing, it fell into my outstretched hands.

The pain of holding it was like holding the sea, like holding a history of immense pain and defiant joy which was not mine but which was now welded to me—not my destiny, not something I was coerced to, not something to which I had been born, predetermined to victory—no, this was my choice. It was my choice to find my center at last, past all failures and fear and missed chances. It was my choice to wait here, just like Semberí had waited once for their star. It had been my choice to catch the seed, and to hold it in my hands out of love. But I could not hold it as I was. It was too much, too vast, and I needed—I needed to match myself to this work.

I am here.

My mind exploded, expanded like wings, embracing the hill, and my broken trees, and the vortex of water below. A new deepname of purest blue ignited in my mind like a beacon, a promise. *Sem.* My other deepnames, too, activated, until I held my full configuration, the Royal House of one, one, and two syllables. Easily, as if I had been singing, I formed a protective triangle around my body, and over the sapphire seed in my hands.

Semberí coalesced before me in their human form. There was barely anything left of them now. A mere hint of a presence. A vapor. "Don't tell Ranra," they whispered hoarsely. "You love her. I don't. She reminds me too much of Ladder. Like him, she is named after ravens and crows . . ."

Even after this great deed and all but gone, they kept to their pettiness. To their pain.

To themself.

"Semberí."

"Keep this a secret from her for a thousand years, until our people are strong again, until a new star is reborn from the seed—"

"Come with me," I said. "Please."

"I cannot. I will dissipate in a moment—but you must go on." There was fear in their voice, and resignation, and a little bit of pride.

I said, "I will help you." This new conviction of mine felt strange, but I did not question it.

After a moment, almost imperceptibly, the ghost nodded.

I breathed. The Royal House expanded in my mind, and easily, so easily, I spun the ghost. They were almost gone, so thin was their substance, but I spun them into a cord of blue vapor, just like Dorod had given me for my token. I could not thread the seed, but I wove the vapor-thread around it like they taught me, into a frame that held the star-seed lovingly in place. That done, I secured the new necklace around my neck. I put the sapphire seed against my bare skin, where it nestled, neither warm nor cold, neither agitated nor calm. A promise, a new story, which I did not yet understand. And perhaps I did not need to.

My new configuration still extended, I ran down the hill like I was flying.

Ranra

Pluck everything, and especially Erígra Lilún, for whom I risked not just my own life, but the lives of others, the lives of all the children and adults who waited for me to steer them away from the dying island of Geu. Dorod had offered to wait for Lilún instead of me, but I sent them on. Those who remained with me did so by choice, wanting to aid me, or out of necessity. I stood on the pier among our discarded treasures, fuming at Lilún, at myself.

The crowd was gone. In the end, we managed to fit everyone who came to the harbor, Those who could sail away did so, either on one of the great ships or on boats big and small. So many of the people refused to believe that the islands were done for, and found shelter where they could, hoping to wait this out. A few more people came, and I found space for them by tossing out some food. It wasn't the best decision, but it was mine.

I kept thinking that I should go look for my mother. Again and again she had refused me. I sent a friend—even now—but they came back empty-handed and wouldn't even look at me. I had failed even in this. Like others, she believed I was lying, or betraying the isles by running away instead of hunkering down to weather the danger.

As I waited, pacing the pier, a cat ran through the deserted harbor and bumped into my feet. It was Gogor, bedraggled, with singed whiskers. I bent to pet him, but he screamed at me, showing a mouthful of teeth.

I said, "I will take you." It was folly, but what else did I have? Add a cat to my tally of failures . . .

Gogor emitted a series of plaintive miaows, and three other cats darted toward us through the debris of the harbor. A striped gray one, thinner and jumpier-looking even than Gogor, and two kittens. I waved them toward the ship, and they dashed past me. My people eyed me, but I shrugged. I had thrown out books, pieces of art, even food. If the weight of these cats was going to drown us, so be it.

We waited. The hill was not that far, and certainly Lilún would not wander around gathering quince and composing poems? I became so angry and so desperate I pulled on my deepnames and amplified my voice to shout my lover's name at the top of my lungs.

Shortly after that, Lilún appeared, running toward me. My breath caught despite all my anger. There was something Birdlike about Lilún, their bleached hair still tightly braided, their eyes alight. Their clothes billowed around them like plumage.

They ran up to me. They looked radiant. Bird's bloody beak radiant. Lilún's magic was engaged, and I saw that they now wielded the Royal House.

"You waited for me!" they exclaimed.

"I will never leave you behind." I said, quite grumpily. "But what in Bird's name happened on that hill?"

Lilún beamed at me. "I have the seed."

"You and your plucking trees."

We clasped each other fiercely, briefly, then rushed onboard. In a short while, we launched.

My elated mood did not last. Though the erams still fought with the sea, I saw multiple vortices opening up, the roiling of the wave exposing rocks I had never seen before. I saw the lava flowing from the Mother coming closer, devouring all in its path, heard the shrill cries of birds and the rumbling of earth and wave.

My Warlord's Triangle engaged, I steered the ship forward. It was animated by both magic and mechanics, and it was strong and responsive to my will, and in any other hour I would have been soaring. Now, I clenched my teeth so tightly I thought my jaw would crack. Tossed by the storm, the grand ship Dorod had built moved away from the pier among the devastation on land and sea. My people, those powerful enough to help in this endeavor, engaged their deepnames on the deck, helping stabilize our course. We were far behind the other ships still, but pulling farther and farther away from land.

Lilún

I felt the moment the star died as an abrupt cessation of sound. Color was leeched from water and land, and only the stark black-and-white images remained, then they, too, froze. The whole world stopped. I could not move a finger. I could not breathe.

Then, just as abruptly, everything rushed back. I looked at our islands, our homeland, beloved for so long. The mountain, unleashed from its tether, was not just erupting—it was breaking apart, cleaved in two by an enormous force, and death spilled from it in a liquid river of red. A humongous scream issued forth from the land, and the island of Geu, my land, my heart, began to sink.

Above the islands I now saw Bird. Each person who died would be visited by Bird, but only the strongest of the living could see her. I had never been able to see her before, but now, with the Royal House, I could. Each dying person saw Bird as their own shape—a cormorant, an owl, a sparrow. The goddess was far enough now that I could only guess at the shapes she took as she came for the dying and the dead. A mountain eagle. A gull. An osprey. Another gull.

I saw more and more Bird shapes as the sea rushed in. The land broke apart, boiling, twisting, screaming, sinking. I could no longer distinguish Bird's shapes, nor was she singular now. She swooped down, all at once, a hundred times, a thousand times, a rain of uncountable Bird shapes coming and coming and coming for my people—until the air was full of Birds, the air sang with her plumage, falling and rising again with their souls. Under my feet, the ship shook, tossed by a violent storm.

By my side, Ranra stifled a scream.

She had just lost her mother, and the mountain, and the star. We all lost so much, too much to absorb yet—but my fathers could still be on some ship, and I had Semberí and the seed right here with me. And I had Ranra. I had to offer her my hope.

I reached over and put a hand on her arm. I expected her to shrug me off, to snarl, but she did not.

I said, "It's time to look."

"Pluck you," she said.

We stood silently, looking out. I thought I saw ghosts in the water, their hands of foam and vapor reaching out toward the ship, then one by one they were licked by the wave. Perhaps it was just my eyes tricking me.

"We must continue," I said. "For them and for us, to wrench meaning out of this. We must survive."

"What if I do not want to survive?" Ranra cried. "The land is lost and all it held. So many people. We failed. I failed."

"This is a story. But there is more than one way to tell it." It had always been hard for me to look people in the eye, but now I held Ranra's gaze. I saw her pain and attended to it. "We failed in many ways, yes. We failed, but we did the work." I was not strong or brave enough to heal the star, but I could reach Ranra. "And now we must continue. We must do the work again, to help those alive, to remember those who did not make it, to build a new home for the children. To plant the seed."

"This is not the time for poetry," she snarled, but I thought that despite her despair, she heard me.

"It is never the time for poetry, and it is always the time," I said. "We must begin again."

Ranra

Wordlessly, I turned away from the isles and faced east, toward the open and turbulent sea. We were catching up with Dorod and the other erams. My dying land was behind. I could only look forward now.

I stretched my arms outward, and with all my might that had failed and failed us again, and all the new might I had taken, I formed a structure of light above my head. The Warlord's Triangle was a closed system. I was alone, connected to nobody, not even to Lilún. This felt right.

I spun the triangle of power above my head, faster and faster, overlaying the images I created with great precision and determination, finally fully grasping the extent of my will.

My people's survival. Only this.

Terein did not think the ships could survive the death of the star, but I was not Terein. My will was as vast and deep as the sea, my will was more power-ful than any storm, my will extended from horizon to horizon, unbroken, triumphant. I cast it upon the tur-bulence of the sea, made structures that lit up the wave with hundreds of threads of light. I did not know ex-actly what I was doing as I invented this new geometry, and my head was breaking into a thousand pieces, but none of it mattered.

And then I was not alone. By my side, Lilún too had

spread their arms and engaged their new Royal House, mimicking my actions. Upon all the ships and the surviving boats, the named strong who had the power of three and two syllables all called on their configurations now, spreading their arms wide like a hundred Birds, not connecting, but creating structures of their own and casting them upon the waves. A sound, like a wordless song, an exhalation, arose from all the ships, from all of us, and kept rising—a keening, a litany, a farewell. A beginning.

What we built was different than before. No more a structure that empowered me and only me, this was a freely woven net we all made, each of us alone and together, now cast upon the unconquerable wave.

Behind us, the islands were sinking. Vortices gaped open to swallow the land and all it held. Living birds cried shrilly as they circled above their lost homes.

But where we passed, the sea was pacified.

None of it was done perfectly. Survivals never were. Later there would be a lifetime in which to grieve, to blame myself for all the failures and the deaths. But that future did not exist yet. Ahead of us lay the vastness of water that separated our Sinking Lands from the core of the landmass—all the unknown and dangerous expanses of the wave. Beyond it somewhere, almost due east and a bit to the north, lay that treacherous, desolate marsh of the Coast, and all its losses and triumphs, its heartbreaks and its stories.

Our arms outstretched, our magics engaged, we steered ourselves toward that future.

Acknowledgements

Several years ago, editor Li Chua accepted my poem "Ranra's Unbalancing" for *Strange Horizons*, one of the oldest and most venerable online SFF publications. The following year, "Ranra's Unbalancing" won the *Strange Horizons* Readers' Poll in the poetry category. Like many of my poems, this one just came to me. In it, Ranra addresses an unnamed person who cares a lot about quince. "Shut up about the quince," she says, but clearly that does not happen.

I kept thinking about the poem, and about its people and its lost land. I promised myself I would write about them one day, but it took a global pandemic and a sudden, tragic passing of a dear friend for this book to become a reality. My friend Corey loved Ranra, and they hoped to read this book one day. I'm sorry I could not finish it sooner. I am not sorry that the book exists. It is a book about endings and failures and at the same time about community, its strengths and its fault lines. I hope this book resonates with you. I hope to write many more. To all who are reading this book and recognize themselves in the ichidi variations, this is for you—no matter if you're out, or questioning, or unsure. Who you are is important.

This work would not be possible without my chosen family of queers at the virtual pub and elsewhere (you know who you are), and all the trans and/or nonbinary and/or queer authors who inspired me, and who shared the joys and the sorrows and the ridiculous moments of the writing journey. Thank you. Many thanks to my spouse Bogi Takács and my child Mati, who are my favorite people to huddle with during a pandemic. Bogi is an incredible reader, and eir support and encouragement helped this book to exist. I hope you seek out eir work.

Many thanks to my publishing team—my intrepid editor Jaymee Goh, as well as the senior editor Jill Roberts, and the publisher Jacob Weisman of Tachyon Publications; my agent Mary C. Moore; the meticulous copyeditor Anne Zanoni; and the graphic designer Elizabeth Story—for your tireless work on this book. Any remaining comma splices are entirely my fault.

Last but not least, I would like to acknowledge my appreciation to three ginger cats who inspired Gogor: the Tachyon office cat Zeppo, whose side does have a swirl; the Wonder Fair store cat Dave, who on many occasions helped me select stationery and pens to work on this book; and finally, the nameless nomad who is claimed by many households, but is very much their own cat about town.

R. B. LEMBERG is a queer, bigender fantasist, poet, and professor. R. B. was born in L'viv, Ukraine, and also lived in subarctic Russia and Israel before migrating to the US. R. B.'s Birdverse novella *The Four Profound Weaves* (Tachyon, 2020) was a finalist for the Nebula, Ignyte, Locus, and World Fantasy awards, as well as an Otherwise Award honoree. They are also a Le Guin Feminist Fellow.

R. B.'s poetry memoir *Everything Thaws* was published by Ben Yehuda Press in 2022. Their stories and poems have appeared in *Lightspeed Magazine*'s *Queers Destroy Science Fiction!, Beneath Ceaseless Skies, We Are Here: Best Queer Speculative Fiction 2020, Sisters of the Revolution: A Feminist Speculative Fiction Anthology,* and many other venues. R. B. lives in Lawrence, Kansas, with their spouse and fellow author Bogi Takács, their child Mati, and all the cumulative books and fountain pens. You can find R.B. on Twitter at @rb_lemberg, on Patreon at http://patreon.com/rblemberg, and at their websites rblemberg.net and birdverse.net.